NEPTUNE'S
TEARS

SUSAN WAGGONER

NEPTUNE'S TEARS

HENRY HOLT AND COMPANY

NEW YORK

Henry Holt and Company, LLC
Publishers since 1866
175 Fifth Avenue
New York, New York 10010
macteenbooks.com

Library of Congress Cataloging-in-Publication Data
Waggoner, Susan.
Neptune's tears / Susan Waggoner.—First edition.
pages   cm
Summary: In 2218 London, seventeen-year-old Zee's plans for a
career as an empath are undermined when she becomes distracted
by feelings for David, an attractive patient who, she learns,
is of an alien race but who has secrets he cannot share.
ISBN 978-0-8050-9677-4 (hardback)—ISBN 978-0-8050-9678-1 (e-book)
[1. Adventure and adventurers—Fiction.   2. Psychic ability—Fiction.
3. Empathy—Fiction.   4. Extraterrestrial beings—Fiction.
5. Love—Fiction.   6. Science fiction.]   I. Title.
PZ7.W1241353Nep 2013   [Fic]—dc23   2013001712

Henry Holt books may be purchased for business or promotional use.
For information on bulk purchases please contact Macmillan Corporate and
Premium Sales Department at (800) 221-7945 x5442 or by e-mail at
specialmarkets@macmillan.com.

First Edition—2013 / Designed by April Ward

Printed in the United States of America

1 3 5 7 9 10 8 6 4 2

NEPTUNE'S
TEARS

CHAPTER ONE

DIVESTING

Zee hesitated for the second it took the blue light to flash green, then passed through the arch and into the Accident & Emergency waiting room. She gave a little wave to Omar at the security desk.

"Hey, pineapple girl," he said. He'd been calling her pineapple girl for three months now, even though her mistaken haircut choice had almost completely grown out. She didn't mind the teasing, though. She could feel his good heart in everything he said.

"Hey, Omar."

"How come you're working Friday night again?"

Zee smiled. "Just lucky, I guess."

"Must be something wrong with boys these days. Friday night, you ought to be out having fun. This the best place you got to go?"

"Looks like." Zee walked on fast to hide her smile, a little embarrassed about liking her job so much. Omar didn't know it, but he'd got it right. This *was* the best place to be on Friday night, at least as far as Zee was concerned.

The room was crowded, and Zee felt the pop and jangle of Friday craziness flowing around her. It would peak just before midnight, then grow fainter and fainter, all the energy and fights and reckless acts exhausting themselves. Friday was a high-wire act that ended in the peacefulness of Saturday morning.

Zee checked her orders as she changed into her scrubs, balancing on one foot as she read the screen inside her locker door. She saw with dismay that Ellie Hart, who'd received new lungs a few months ago, had been readmitted with an infection and extreme exhaustion. Also a high white blood cell count and enzyme levels that didn't look good. A sudden heaviness flooded Zee's chest. Sadness.

Everyone knew you weren't supposed to have favorite patients, but everyone also knew that sometimes it couldn't be helped. Zee and Mrs. Hart had hit it off immediately, maybe because, like Zee, Mrs. Hart was an

American living in London, or maybe because they'd been born exactly one hundred years apart. Zee thought it had more to do with Mrs. Hart herself. At their first session, she had been sitting up in bed, wearing the usual hospital gown and what looked like a gajillion diamonds. At her throat, in her ears, on both wrists, and Zee even thought she saw a twinkle or two gleaming in her hair.

"Gaudy, aren't they?" Mrs. Hart asked with a smile. "I hope you don't mind. They're my good luck charms."

Zee could not imagine owning so many diamonds. Maybe Mrs. Hart had read in some book that diamonds had healing properties and rented them. People showed up for sessions with all kinds of mistaken notions. Zee looked at the diamonds again. They had a faint, radiant golden glow, as if sunlight were buried within them. "Are they real?"

Mrs. Hart chuckled, a good sign in someone who'd just had replacement surgery. "Heavens, no. The originals are far too valuable and don't belong to me anyway. But the settings are real. I designed them."

"No way."

"Yes, way," Mrs. Hart said, extending an arm encircled with bracelets. "Touch," she invited.

Zee did and instantly felt a surge of joy. Joy and something more. What was it? She closed her eyes. It was complex, as tangled as a ball of yarn.

"My first big success as a jewelry designer," Mrs. Hart explained. "And my last. The Neptune diamonds."

Zee jerked her hand away. Of course. The golden glow should have tipped her off. Everyone knew about the Neptune diamonds, diamonds drenched in sunlight and tragedy.

"It's all right, dear. I designed these settings before anything went wrong. They're not . . . that is, I don't think they absorbed . . . umm . . . how would you put it?"

Ninety years before Zee was born, the first generation of robots was sent into space. Zee still remembered how the hologram of the pale blue rocket had leapt out of her social studies book and vanished into the ceiling with a puff of vapor. She loved holos, and that had been an especially good one, so clear she could see *Tiffany* written on the rocket's side.

Certain there might be precious gems out there, the famous jeweler had funded a twelve-year mission to Neptune. Without the frailty of the human body or emotions to interfere, the bots endured the tedium of the long voyage and functioned perfectly in Neptune's poisonous methane atmosphere—an atmosphere that, as Tiffany's scientists had predicted, rained diamonds. The bots filled a small module with them, launched it on a path back to Earth, and started to build a collection colony.

On Earth, Tiffany held a contest to see who could design the most beautiful rings, necklaces, bracelets, and earrings. Ellie Hart, a newlywed, won.

A few years later, things began to go wrong. The robots, though designed to withstand Neptune's atmosphere, started breaking down. All the systems failed, but none failed all at once or in any predictable way. Instead of going about their tasks until their chips crashed, the bots attempted to repair each other. It became clear that they'd formed friendships and alliances. Their messages back to Earth were full of sadness, and they appeared to care about what was happening to their friends just as much, if not more, than they cared about what happened to themselves.

They gave every appearance of having become human.

Though they are not human! the spokesman holo in Zee's textbook had insisted. *What looks to us like friendship is a programming error. We gave the bots too much freedom to adapt. All that's needed is a little tweak to future models. . . .* Zee was no more convinced than anyone had been at the time. What was human? How could the scientist be sure?

By the time the sample module of Neptune diamonds reached Earth, the last of the robots had fallen silent. All had spent the last hours of their existence fulfilling the mission, making sure at least one shipment of diamonds was sent back to Earth. The diamonds had become Neptune's Tears. Two sets of Mrs. Hart's designs were made. The one with the real diamonds was put on display under bulletproof glass with a plaque that read TO HEROES. The other set was fitted with fakes and given to Mrs. Hart. Mrs. Hart's were awfully good imitations, Zee thought. Whoever had made them even managed to replicate the unique champagne sparkle of the real thing. People were still trying to replicate the shade, or hunting for it in the diamond-rich mountains of the Antarctic Ocean, but no one had succeeded. Zee wondered who had made these.

Zee looked at Mrs. Hart, suddenly understanding the tangle of emotions she'd sensed earlier. "Disappointment," she said. "These became bad luck designs, didn't they? You never got to go to New York, even though nothing that happened was your fault." For a split second, Zee felt the weight of Mrs. Hart's disappointment. "That's so unfair!"

"It was a long time ago now. Almost a hundred years. And these fakes have been my good luck charms all this time, more than you'll ever know." She shook her bangles as if clearing the air. "Well, I'd say you're more than up to your job. Shall we get started?"

Zee wished she'd been on duty tonight when Mrs. Hart was readmitted. With divesting and two or three patients to see first, it would be two A.M. before Zee got to Mrs. Hart's room.

Mrs. Hart would be sleeping when their session began, which was fine from a treatment standpoint, but Zee wouldn't get to talk to her.

She looked at the rest of her patient list. Caroline Neville was back as well. Zee needed to talk to her supervisor about that, because there was really nothing wrong with Caroline except that she was lonely on Friday nights. Zee touched the screen again to see if there were any requests from her patients. Mrs. Hart asked her to think of a lake at dusk with loons calling across it. A new patient, a boy who'd had a leg grown to replace the one he lost from the knee down, asked if she could please imagine him running the 400-meter race at his school's Sports Day and being the first to cross the finish line.

This was why Zee loved working with kids. They had a gift for healing. His parents had probably reminded him that first he'd have to learn to walk again, or told him that winning was a *team* effort. But little Antoine with the budding leg had asked for just the right thing.

Sometimes you *did* have to run before you could walk, at least in your heart.

Finished, Zee touched the screen one more time, and it turned back into a mirror. Her eyes appeared where names and charts had been. Her hair! It took two hands to gather it back, and even then a few spiraling strands escaped. She tried tucking them in, without much luck. It wasn't long enough yet. That pineapple cut really *had* been a mistake. She snapped a band around it, then slid her ID over her head, making sure the sensors in the cord touched the skin on the back of her neck. Two years training, one interning, and she still felt the tickle of excitement when the sensors made contact and her name tag began to glow with the soft, optimistic blue of her profession: *Zee McAdams, Empath.*

Zee pushed through the double doors marked DIVESTING and entered a long, quiet corridor where the light gradually changed from white to shadowy blues and greens. It was like wading into a tranquil pool, the colors reaching first up to her knees, then her waist and shoulders. Another twenty-five yards, and she began to feel like a tadpole swimming beneath a canopy of lily pads.

She had mastered divesting faster than most. In

the beginning, it could take interns hours to divest, but Zee had seldom taken more than an hour. And once she divested, she hung on to it. She didn't get distracted, and she'd never boomeranged, snapping back into herself. Everyone in her class envied her for catching on so fast, but Zee thought it was probably just because she was young and not much had happened to her.

In the divesting room, she found an empty pod, chose her light levels, and programmed sounds and images. Some empaths liked to lie down, some preferred sitting cross-legged on the floor. An ordinary table and chair worked fine for Zee. She dropped her arms to her sides, closed her eyes, and let her head tip forward like a heavy flower. Then she began building the healing bridge, the invisible waves of energy that connected her to each of her patients and would, over the course of her shift, draw her to each of them in turn. No two empaths built their bridges in exactly the same way. Zee's started with magic beans tossed into the darkness and a quick flurry of vines and leaves, different-colored vines for each patient. When the vines began to glow, a drift of sparkling mist almost always appeared. Zee felt her shoulder, elbow, and wrist joints— oranges, lemons, and limes—grow heavy, and all the things that were her daily self began to flow away through her fingertips.

Forty minutes later, just as she set out for the pediatric wing, Piper Simms caught up with her. "Dr. Morgan wants you in A&E exam two," Piper said.

Zee didn't like to talk to anyone between the time she finished divesting and the time she saw her first patient. Too much of herself might bubble back into the space she'd created.

"Can it wait? I'm on my way to a new patient. Leg bud."

"The leg's been reassigned." Piper flashed her handheld for Zee to see the orders screen. "To me."

There was no need to look so triumphant about it, Zee thought.

Three years ago, when Zee had started her training, Piper had been the best empath in the unit. Now she was struggling with burnout and seemed to resent each new class of empaths that came along, Zee in particular. Piper's flashes of meanness were so frequent that Zee had talked to her adviser about them.

"Empath envy," the adviser explained. "Piper knows you can become as good an empath as she was."

"But I make mistakes. I miss so many things." Zee paused a moment. "Why did you say 'was'?"

"What?"

"Was. You said I could be as good as she *was*."

"Ah." Her adviser became thoughtful. "Well. Piper's three years older than you and suffering an affliction hazardous to all empaths. She's fallen in love."

It was the first time Zee had ever heard how deeply personal attachments could affect her work. Strong emotions, hate as well as love, could derail an empath's ability to concentrate. Zee felt truly sorry for Piper.

"Will she ever get it back? I mean, if she gets married and that's all settled and taken care of, will she be best again?"

"Some can do that," the adviser said. "Some wash out, and some struggle with it all their lives. There's no way of predicting. Piper will always be a good, even gifted, empath. But as good as she was? Time will tell. In the meantime, always try to be gentle with an empath who's suffering. It could be you someday."

Zee didn't think so. She had no intention of falling in love—especially now. She had raced back to the dorm to tell the others what she'd learned. And was embarrassed to discover that everyone knew but her, because everyone else had already been in love, and love, they explained, was just the highest form of piercing. Zee knew about piercing, the disturbing phenomenon of being so overwhelmed by attraction to someone that you lost your focus. Zee had felt attraction, but never the piercing they described. When someone else was all you could think of, or you found yourself wearing his T-shirt under your scrubs so you could feel him around you all during your shift, you'd been pierced.

"But that's against the rules," Zee said when she heard about the T-shirt. The hospital had a dress code for everyone.

"Yes it is," Mariko Sanchez said. "But you do it anyway. That's how you know you've been pierced."

Zee had tried to be patient with Piper ever since, but right now it wasn't easy.

"Don't you think you'd better get going?" Piper asked. "Dr. Morgan asked for you especially."

Zee didn't argue. Once you started your shift, you had no personal opinions. And Piper, in her present state, would probably report her if she protested.

"All right," Zee said at last. "I haven't had any A&Es since Wednesday, so it will be a change of pace."

"You're *so* not kidding it will," Piper said behind her in a chilly, sunken voice Zee was certain she hadn't been meant to hear.

CHAPTER TWO

CLOSE ENCOUNTERS

Zee didn't know what she'd find in A&E. She hoped it wasn't severed body parts. Blood always made her queasy, and a severed part made the whole body angry and difficult to work with.

Dr. Morgan was waiting for her with a grim look on his face, but that didn't mean anything, because Dr. Morgan *always* had a grim look on his face. Except when the problem turned out to be routine. Then he looked disappointed.

"Gash to forehead," he said, steering Zee toward A&E2. "Refused a head scan and now wants to check out AMA."

Against medical advice. Yes, that would certainly annoy Dr. Morgan.

"Do you think he has a concussion?" she asked.

"I think he has a subdural hematoma. It could blow like Vesuvius any minute." His eyes sparkled with anticipation as he gestured toward the door of the examining room. "See if you can keep him here."

Zee took a clearing breath and entered the room. The young man sitting in the cubicle wasn't that much older than she was. Zee had been trained to notice the small gestures that took place in the first few minutes of an encounter, revealing the patient's state of mind and openness to noninvasive healing. She got the impression that the young man had been rubbing a small metal bar against his forehead, but it disappeared into his pocket so swiftly she couldn't be certain.

When he lifted his head, Zee felt a tug. Involuntary personal attraction. A reflex, like coughing when you walked into a dusty room. She'd felt it before with other patients and knew how to dismiss it. It was a sign, though, that Piper had created more than a tiny pinprick in her calm. She was determined to get it back.

"Hi," she said, "I'm Zee."

"I'm David Sutton, about to check out." But instead of hopping off the hospital trolley, he stayed where he was. Everything around him seemed to stop, and the room floated into stillness, like a leaf or a feather settling to Earth. For a long moment, he simply stared at her, and Zee allowed him to, without moving or closing her face to him.

It wasn't easy to let someone look at you like that, but many patients seemed to need to. "Like someone taking a car for a road test," their instructor had explained during training, "only you're the car." They'd laughed, but that didn't make it easier. Five in her class had washed out because they could not be looked at without posturing or fidgeting. At first, Zee had felt so naked standing before a patient she'd had to distract herself by making lists of song titles that started with certain letters of the alphabet, or by wondering why two-hundred-year-old movies like *Titanic* were often better than the hologram remakes. Now that she was more confident, she'd begun to use these small capsules of time to begin building a healing bridge to the patient.

But that wasn't happening tonight. She was having trouble reestablishing her calm and felt as naked as she had the first time she'd been with a patient. No sooner had she dropped the foundations of the bridge into place and sent invisible blue vines twining through the air than they crumbled and vanished from her mind.

David Sutton's eyes were still on her, curious and

sea gray beneath dark eyebrows. She felt her skin grow warm and tried to think of song titles that began with the letter *A*. She drew a blank, so she moved on to the letter *B*. "Bitter Poison," "Borrowed Time," "Been Around and Down," "Boomdance." It usually took patients less than thirty seconds to satisfy themselves, but more than a minute passed, and Zee still felt his gaze.

Suddenly, he smiled. "You're one of us," he said.

Now what was *that* supposed to mean? Maybe Dr. Morgan was right—he really *did* have a subdural hematoma, and his brain was already starting to suffer from hypoxia. Or did he mean that he was also an empath? That would explain the ribbon of energy she'd begun to feel pulsing between them.

He spoke again in a voice that was almost a whisper, the words such a quick, soft rush she could not even tell what language they might be.

This was not going according to plan at all, and she tried to steer it back. "Dr. Morgan thought we might talk for a few minutes."

"Great. I'll just get my stuff and we can go. Is there a coffee shop around here?"

Okay. So he wasn't so weird after all, just flirty. She'd had lots of practice handling flirts and worse than flirts.

"Dr. Morgan wanted me to make sure you're all right. According to your chart, you were unconscious when they brought you in, with quite a wound on your forehead."

He looked confused. "Who are you again?"

Did he not see the glowing blue of her badge? "Zee McAdams. I'm your empath this evening. I can help you with the wound on your head."

Suddenly, there was a wrenching in the energy field. He jerked his whole torso backward, as if taking himself out of reach. The light she'd felt between them, or thought she'd felt, was gone.

"A mind reader? No thanks. If I want my fortune told, there's a carnival on the other side of town."

"I don't read minds," she explained. She'd had this conversation too many times to count, but usually it was with older patients who thought psychic healing was a scheme to pump up their hospital bills.

"No?" he challenged.

"No. I read bodies."

"Aren't you people always saying that the mind and the body are one?"

That was true enough. The mind and the body were one, in ways that even science didn't fully understand. She shouldn't have said she read bodies. It wasn't technically true. What she did, both consciously and subconsciously, was make an infinite number of tiny observations and allow a pattern to emerge, a pattern that guided the healing energy she sent back to the patient.

"I'm only here to help you, and it won't hurt a bit." She took a step toward him and extended her hand. "According to your chart, we really should make sure about that wound—"

"Stay *away* from me," he said, raising both hands, as if ready to push her back.

Zee stopped. She shouldn't have taken that last step or extended her hand. Now she'd lost the patient. "Sorry. It's just that you *were* brought in unconscious, and Dr. Morgan wants to—"

"Have a look around inside my head. I get that. But I'm leaving anyway."

Zee bit her lip. If he left and collapsed in the street, it would be her fault.

"Look," he said. "I'm fine. No, really *look*. Do you see a wound on my forehead?"

"Well, not exactly, but—"

But there had been one there before. Hadn't there? She realized he was still staring at her. In fact, his eyes hadn't really left her since she'd entered the room. She felt the tug of attraction again. This time, in spite of the disastrous way things were going, it wasn't so easy to dismiss. When she tried, exactly the opposite happened. She felt herself come flowing completely back and knew that, for the first time ever, she'd have to return to the unit and redivest before she could see another patient.

And of course she'd have to write up a full report of everything that had happened, which would be tricky, because she wasn't at all sure what had happened. Was it David Sutton's steady gaze? The way his arms looked strong but gentle at the same time and made her wonder what his hand would feel like touching her? And the energy pulse she thought she'd felt between them? It was too embarrassing to contemplate. She couldn't even mention her suspicion that Piper's competitiveness was behind it all. Piper had finagled good cases away from her before, and Zee could just picture her telling Dr. Morgan that Zee was *so much better* with difficult patients than she herself was, and that she wouldn't mind swapping cases if that's what was best for the patient.

Zee glanced at David Sutton. "Can I ask you a question?"

"Sure."

"Why do you keep looking at me like that? Have you seen me before? Have I done something . . . ?"

"No, nothing like that," he said. "It's your hair."

"Oh." Zee raised her hand to tuck the usual stray strands behind her ears and realized she'd lost her band; her tangled auburn curls had come loose. So that was it. Her hair often took people by surprise, but not so much that they stared at her so long. His rudeness made her feel like a zoo animal.

"It's not like I'm the *only* redhead left, you know. There are almost a hundred thousand of us. It's a recessive gene, not an extinct one. Haven't you ever seen a holo of a redhead at least? Zeesh. What planet are you from?"

David Sutton stood up, a graceful unfolding that made her realize how tall he was. "You call it Gliese 581 C." he answered. "We call it Omura. Or didn't Dr. Morgan tell you?"

CHAPTER THREE

THE DAY
THEY LANDED

Zee flew down the corridor so fast she felt cool air against her face. An *alien*? How had *that* happened? There were few things in the world Zee truly disliked— she had even learned not to recoil at the sight of stewed tomatoes on the breakfast table of her residence hall— but the idea of aliens still spooked her. And even though she'd never actually met one, she'd always been sure she'd know right away.

And now exactly the opposite had happened. No matter how fast she walked, she couldn't forget the moment of *connection* between them. She felt tricked into opening herself to someone who didn't belong here, whose civilization's arrival she held responsible for ruining her father's life.

Zee didn't slow her pace until she passed through the double doors of the empaths' unit. Home safe. She paused and took a deep, forgetting breath.

The aquatic blue lights had just begun to calm her when she saw Piper's dark, seal-like head bent over the circular main desk. Hadn't Piper been on her way to work with Antoine, her leg bud patient? Learning that Zee had been attracted to David Sutton would just be the frosting on Piper's cake, Zee realized, and tried to hurry past the desk without attracting attention. But it was useless. She felt the heat of a blush creeping up her throat and into her cheeks, where they burned like twin bonfires. Piper noticed right away.

"Why, Zee!" The look of concern on Piper's face, like the sugar sweetness in her voice, was false. "Are you all right? Is something wrong?"

"I'm fine," Zee answered, sounding a lot less casual than she'd hoped. She lifted her chin a little. "I'm fine."

Piper raised her eyebrows and let the obvious question float in the air. *If you're fine, why are you back here redivesting?* When she spoke, her voice was edged with a frill of sarcasm, "I'm glad you're fine, Zee. Because if I didn't know better, I'd say you'd been pierced."

Zee refused to acknowledge the comment. "Aren't you supposed to be working with my leg bud patient?" she asked.

"Just getting some additional input," Piper said breezily, slipping her handheld into her pocket. "Have a great shift."

Zee could almost see the smirk beneath Piper's smile. But as she started down the corridor to redivest, that wasn't what bothered her. What bothered her was the thought that, for all the mocking exaggeration, Piper was actually right. She had been pierced. By an alien.

✦⁓ ✦

The aliens arrived the summer Zee was six, just before school began. She didn't even know what aliens were back then, but she would remember that weekend for the rest of her life. It was the first time she'd ever noticed that the world was bigger than herself and her parents and their friends. Bigger and quite a bit different. Until then, she'd thought the whole world was the way her world was.

They'd spent the weekend working, as they almost always did, at a Woodstock revival festival. Her parents were professional reenactors, living history, and Woodstock was their specialty. To Zee, it seemed the most natural thing in the world for her mother and father to wear patched bell-bottom jeans and raspberry-tinted wire-rim glasses and slide back in time to relive an event that had happened more than two centuries ago. It was in their blood and part of their romance, because they had first met at Woodstock 200, the bicentennial, when her mother was four and her father was five. According to both of Zee's grandmothers, her father had given Zee's mother a handful of pretty weeds and said, "I like you. Do you want to get married?" And her mother had said, soberly, "I'm not getting married until I'm nine. And we have to have banana ice pops." They met again at the same festival twenty years later and fell in love for real. It was the most romantic story Zee knew and part of the reason she had always been so certain she could never be pierced. She was waiting for a story like that of her own.

The weekend the aliens came, her mother wore a long, billowy gown with tiny mirrors sewn all over it. While her father was onstage singing, her mother sold T-shirts tie-dyed to look like sunsets and starry explosions and galaxies in collision. Zee's job was to fold up the T-shirts people bought and put them in a bag with a sprinkle of what her mother called "good karma"— dried pink petals that forever after would make Zee think *good karma* whenever she smelled a rose. It was

Sunday, and just when the sun was beginning to slant and things should have been winding down, an electric jolt went through the crowd. It started by a booth where antique radios blared and fanned out from there. Some people screamed, others cheered or began to cry. Zee didn't know if something good had happened or something bad. Onstage, her father's band stopped playing. Someone holding an old-fashioned transistor radio to his ear took the microphone and said, "How far out is this, man? They're here! The president just made a special announcement! They're finally here! The aliens, man. The aliens are on the White House lawn!"

When Zee's father finally made his way through the crowd to Zee and her mother, he had a huge smile on his face. He talked about portals opening and the Age of Aquarius being here at last. Then he scooped Zee up and said, "You'll see it all, Zee. Wonderful things are going to happen. These people have the answers. An end to war. Energy that never runs out. How to travel all over the universe. And they're here to tell us about it."

All the way home, her father talked about the things that would happen now. He was full of plans—for himself, for Zee, for their whole family. He kept telling Zee that she was going to grow up in a whole different world. "What the heck. Now that the door to galactic travel has been blasted wide open, we might pick up stakes and move to another planet!"

"Earl!" her mother said. "You're scaring her."

"No I'm not. Am I, princess?"

Zee remembered shaking her head no—she wasn't scared because his smile was so sweet she wanted it to go on forever.

She often wished she could go back in time, grab that day, and shake it until it came out the way her father wanted it to. She wished she could protect him from all the disappointment that was to come.

Because, in the end, the aliens disappointed almost everyone. For thousands of years, people had been wondering if they existed and trying to imagine what they would look like if they did. The one thing people agreed on was that the aliens would look *alien*.

Instead, the aliens looked like humans, only slightly taller. This, they said, confirmed what Omura's genetic scientists had long suspected. After studying Earth for over a hundred years from afar, Omuran scientists became convinced that the planets had been seeded with the same intelligent life forms long ago by an unseen hand. But whereas climatic instability had forced Omurans to concentrate on survival-based technology, Earth's gentler climate had promoted a culture rich in literature, painting, and other arts.

The aliens who arrived were not scientists. They no more understood the technology of their spacecraft than Earthlings did, for it had been designed by Omura's engineers and ran on self-generating software. Asking them to explain how it worked would be like asking a passenger to explain the intricacies of suborbital flight. Instead, their education had focused on Earth languages and culture. They had been sent to study what Omura did not have—works that were created for pleasure and awareness rather than for survival. All they wanted was library cards, museum passes and—most of all—to come and go as they liked and to be left alone, privileges for which they were willing to pay host governments in gold.

America was the first country to accept their offer, but France, England, and Sweden soon did the same. Over the course of Zee's lifetime, the numbers of aliens had grown, and now they could be found in almost every country. True to their word, they kept to themselves and seemed to have little interest in Earthlings.

"They're only making sure we're trustworthy," Zee's father often said. "When they know us better, they'll share their wisdom with us, and their technology."

Others weren't so trusting. Some insisted it was only a matter of time until they unzipped their human suits and revealed the scheming alien within. For most people, though, the protests against them and calls to send them back into space that had been common at first gradually settled into a kind of low-grade irritation. The strange thing was that, since few people knew an alien or had anything to do with them, this irritation was often turned toward people like Zee's father. No one wanted to hear about his belief that the aliens would one day share their great knowledge with the people of Earth. For hundreds of thousands of years, humans had thought of themselves as special. Not only did they not want to be reminded that they weren't unique, it was depressing to think that their Omuran relatives were so far ahead of them. Old friends of her parents stopped calling. There were whispers that her father *wanted* the aliens to take over.

"It's all right, Zee," her father would say. "It's just an opinion. Everyone has a right to their opinion."

But Zee saw how grateful her father was to those who did visit, and it made her want to cry. Just as she wanted to cry when she saw that her father's endless talking about the aliens ruined her mother's happiness. Zee regretted that her little sister, born the year after the Landing, would never know their parents as they had been before, for Zee realized that her father's life had come to a stop that day. So had millions of other lives. All over the world, people were waiting to see what the aliens would do, waiting to find out if it was the end of the world or the beginning. Waiting their lives away. It didn't matter whether the aliens planned to take over or not. They had done enough damage just by arriving.

By the time Zee finished redivesting, it was well after three A.M. Once she got past Piper, redivesting hadn't been as bad as she'd expected. In fact, she felt relaxed and strong with energy as she headed to Ellie Hart's room. She pictured herself walking along a healing bridge of blue vines. Beneath the bridge, a pair of loons sang, their rippling calls to each other forming a bridge of their own. It was as if the first part of her shift had never happened at all. Zee was relieved to discover that there were no lingering effects from the piercing.

As soon as she stepped into the room, a sense of deep, still peace swept forward to meet her. Mrs. Hart was asleep, of course, but Zee could navigate easily by the dim glow of machines and monitors. Moving quietly, she drew a chair alongside the bed and took the old woman's hand in her own.

Zee started, as she always did, by thanking the universe for the gift that had been given to her and asking for the strength to use it well. Then, as Mrs. Hart had asked, she began to imagine a wide blue lake sparkling in the summer sun. She filled the air with the calls of loons and the laughter of Mrs. Hart's children playing near a dock. For good measure, she added the sound of a boat as Mrs. Hart's husband, young and vibrant, started the engine. Who's for water skiing? he called out. Mrs. Hart was lucky to have such good memories.

Next came the part Zee liked best. She pictured Mrs. Hart in all the phases of her life. Learning to walk, blowing out birthday candles, nervous the first time a boy flirted with her. She pictured a young girl sketching necklaces and earrings and pins and bracelets, eager to create things that would make others feel pretty or happy. She pictured a young married woman, then an older Mrs. Hart dancing at her daughter's wedding and asking her husband, Where did all the time go? And from each of these Mrs. Harts, cartwheeling through the seasons and the years, she asked for a bit of health and vitality. Zee didn't understand the flow of time any better than the aliens did, but she believed you were always the selves you had been in the past and would be in the future, and with enough effort, you could reach backward and forward to get help when you needed it.

Time vanished for Zee. She was completely lost in the crowd of Mrs. Harts. Not all patients were so easy to work with. Mrs. Hart was different, and different from the last time she had been here, as if she'd added an extra spiritual dimension.

Zee gathered the energy from all the Mrs. Harts and channeled it to the woman asleep in the bed. She sent it spinning into her brain and heart, let it flow through her arteries, and imagined it settling into her organs, to chase away any infection that might be there.

Then without warning, Zee was gripped by a deep, stabbing pain beneath her rib cage, a pain so intense it was a spasm, lifting her from her chair. She'd only felt this twice before, once with a simulator during training, once with a real patient a year ago.

"*Oh, no,*" she gasped in a whisper. "*No. No. No.*" But Zee knew she was already defeated.

There was no mistaking the throb of a deep and spreading cancer within the fragile old body. From the location of the pain and the enzyme levels she'd read earlier, Zee was fairly certain it was lodged in Mrs. Hart's liver, one of a handful of cancers medicine had not yet found a cure for.

Tears stung Zee's eyes. Two spilled down her cheek in a cold trickle, and she quickly wiped them away. An empath was never to cry in front of a patient, even a sleeping one. Zee struggled for control, but it was no use. Her head bent slowly forward until her face was hidden in the comfort of the soft hospital blanket. It was unprofessional, but she couldn't help herself. The pain in her midriff kept her pinned to her chair, and she could no longer hold back her tears. She wondered if the doctors knew yet, and if anyone had told Mrs. Hart.

She was barely aware, at first, of the gentle hand that came to rest on the top of her head, but she recognized Mrs. Hart's voice.

"It's all right, dear," the old woman said. "You mustn't cry so. I've known for a while now, before I even checked in, and I'm not upset, so don't you be either. I've had a wonderful life, and you won't understand this until you're old yourself, but I'm tired. I'm ready to move on. Besides, how else will I see my husband again?"

Mrs. Hart was right. Zee *didn't* understand. Why Mrs. Hart? Why anyone? Why couldn't everyone just live forever? All she could do was squeeze the old woman's hand. Ellie Hart's answering squeeze was strong and comforting and, against the odds, made Zee feel just a little bit better.

That was the end of Zee's shift. Empaths weren't allowed to redivest twice in one night. Zee explained the situation to the supervisor on duty as briefly as possible, skimming over the encounter with David Sutton and emphasizing instead what had happened with Mrs. Hart. She knew she'd have to make a much longer, more detailed report to her personal supervisor later and dreaded it, but she'd work through it somehow. For now, she was just glad to change back into her street clothes.

It was odd to find the sun just coming up outside. The night had seemed so long that Zee wouldn't have been surprised to step out into a whole different season. But the world was quiet, and it was still summer. She sat for a while on a bench across from the hospital's small garden, watching birds shower themselves with morning dew. How was it that those birds would be alive next year but Mrs. Hart would not?

For the first time in years, Zee felt homesick. Her empath training had taken her away from home early, when she was just thirteen. Her parents hadn't protested, and Zee always wondered if they knew that part of her had begun to be embarrassed by her father's insistence that world peace was what would cause the aliens finally, at last, to share their wisdom. She hoped they also realized how much she loved them and that the only thing strong enough to pull her away from them so early was her desire to be an empath.

Now she felt drained and alone, and she wanted

nothing more than to find herself in the house she grew up in, listening to her father enthuse about the aliens and helping her mother scramble eggs for breakfast while her little sister, Bex, complained about the *humongous, horrendous, hellacious* amount of homework they gave in the fourth grade. The realization that she was far from home made Zee start to cry all over again. She searched her purse for a tissue, but of course she didn't have one. She never did. All that was there was her wallet, some lip gloss, her email stick, and half a chocolate bar.

"I came to apologize."

Zee's head jerked up. There he was. Him. David Sutton. The alien. For a brief, furious instant, she wanted to blame him for Mrs. Hart's illness.

"Go away," she said.

He noticed the tears on her cheeks.

"Gosh, I knew I was rude, but I didn't know it was this bad. You're the first Earth girl I've ever made cry. Here." He handed her a huge, old-fashioned handkerchief and sat down beside her. When Zee didn't stop crying, he went on. "This is worse than I thought. There's only one remedy I can think of."

Zee knew she should excuse herself and walk away, but her curiosity got the upper hand. "What's that?"

"Breakfast," he said, getting to his feet. "If you're

going to cry like that, you need something to eat. Can't I buy you some beans on toast? Or Weetabix?"

He smiled suddenly, a slightly crooked smile, because there was a small scar at the left corner of his mouth. It surprised her to realize aliens could get hurt too. She'd assumed they were invulnerable.

"There's a café down the street. What do you say? I was only kidding about the beans on toast. Actually, I think they have omelets or even bacon sandwiches."

Zee felt the tug of personal attraction all over again. And the pangs of hunger. She'd missed her dinner break because of the redivesting.

"Orange juice too?"

"Whatever you want."

Attraction to an alien? There was a no-fly zone for you. Absolutely the last thing she needed. Except that, just now, it seemed to be exactly what she wanted. A little bit dangerous, a little bit unknown. Just this once, she told herself. Just this once. She might even find out their real reason for being here.

CHAPTER FOUR

THE SHOCK BOMB

The minute Zee stepped into the corridor, she saw her friend Rani's silhouette framed against the window—the *only* window on the ground floor of their residence hall that opened directly to the outside. "A perfect opportunity for sneaking boys in," Rani always said, "and you've got the room right next to it." Then Rani would cross her arms and shake her head disapprovingly, even though the corners of her mouth were turned up in a smile. "What a waste!"

Seeing Rani's impatient silhouette, Zee recalled what their personality tests said about each of them and their likely relationship patterns. Rani could date and flirt with a lot of boys and never take their sighs of heartbreak seriously. Zee was another story. She wasn't the flirt Rani was, but her attachments, once formed, could run deep enough to cause distraction. "It's something of a concern to us," the evaluator had said with a slight frown. Zee remembered the quick flush that had warmed her cheeks. She'd felt accused of something she hadn't done, something she wanted to tell the evaluator wouldn't happen in a thousand years. Instead she'd managed to listen patiently as the evaluator warned her that counseling might be necessary.

In the end, the three who'd been roommates together in the junior program—Zee, Rani, and Jasmine—had not only been among the fifty percent admitted to the senior program but had all completed it with honors. And even though Jasmine had taken a job in her native Indonesia, they were still as close as sisters.

Rani's impatient sigh brought Zee's attention back. "Well? What's the story?"

For a frozen moment, Zee thought Rani was asking about David Sutton. But how could Rani know? "I—"

Rani was always the first person she wanted to tell things to, but right now, standing in the hallway with Rani's bright, inquisitive eyes on her, she found herself pushing David deeper into a protective corner of herself.

"Don't tell me you forgot, Zee! Menthol Light is playing at Blue Elm. Joshua's got four passes." Rani held up four fingers. "Me. Joshua. Joshua's friend Tarquin. You? You said you'd let me know. You even said you kind of liked Tarquin."

Zee did kind of like Tarquin. *Had* kind of liked him. "Sorry, Rani, I just don't feel like it."

Suddenly, Rani pressed the back of her hand against Zee's forehead. "Oh my gosh, you're burning up."

Was she? Zee was just thinking she felt cold. Cold and a little empty, the way she'd felt when David found her outside the hospital. He'd made her feel warm and hopeful for a while, and now it had seeped away. All she really wanted was to get inside her room, lie down under her floating duvet, and find that warmth again.

"You must be coming down with something," Rani said. "Maybe you'd better get to bed. I'll get someone else for Tarquin. And if you feel better later, call me. We'll scare up an extra pass someplace."

Zee's two tranquil rooms in the residence hall had never looked more welcoming. The hall had once been four separate buildings bordering Ford Square, an old-fashioned block of green grass and trees not far from the hospital. Several years ago, the buildings had been joined together and the square roofed over and climate controlled, a private front yard where peonies and roses always bloomed. Often when she came off a shift she would wander out there barefoot, letting the cool green grass relax her from the toes up.

But this morning was different. Zee tapped a panel, and the window cycled to sunset and nightfall and then to a blank, midnight blue. She noticed the email stick on her nightstand pulsing with color, picked it up, pointed it at the wall, and scrolled through her mail. She opened the one from Jasmine in Indonesia. It began *Remember the new intern I told you about? Raj? We've had three dates now and are driving to the beach this weekend*—and went on to take up most of the wall. Zee opened the hologram attachment, and there was Raj. He looked nice, handsome even, but she couldn't help comparing him with David. Don't be so lame, she told herself. She would never see David Sutton again, so thinking about him was a waste of time. She clicked the stick to close the email. *Save attachment?* No. She'd always thought there was something creepy in saving holos of people you didn't know. Especially other people's boyfriends.

Zee peeled out of her clothes and dropped her favorite four-sizes-too-big tee over her head, then slid into bed and pressed the bedside panel that dimmed the bedroom walls. Finally, she pulled the pale yellow floating duvet over her. She found the corner tab and pressed the upper left of the square twice. Instantly, the duvet lifted and formed a cocoon around her, leaving a two-centimeter margin of free space. She pressed the upper right part of the square and felt the envelope of space that surrounded her fill with gentle, warming air. And then she let herself begin to think about David Sutton.

Against all odds, he'd made her laugh.

First, though, he'd brought her back to the world of the living. By the time he'd found Zee outside the hospital, the knowledge that Mrs. Hart was dying had spread inside her like a cold, deep lake. On the short walk from the hospital to the café, she was sure he'd seen her shivering once or twice. She liked that he didn't ask her what was wrong, just directed them to cross from the shady side of the street to the side that was in the sun.

At the café, he picked a booth away from the door and motioned for her to slide in. "It's better if you sit first. My legs kind of take up the rest." He looked embarrassed, but it was true. When he slid in across from her, his knees almost touched her side of the booth.

He must have seen her eyes widen when a waitress went by with a tray of double hot chocolate Krakatoa Mochas, a house specialty. "Let's ditch plan A and have those," he said. "With extra . . . hmmmm . . . extra whatever."

She reminded herself that just a few minutes ago she'd been intent on uncovering his real reason for being on the planet. Could a man with marshmallow froth at the corners of his mouth be up to anything truly sinister? Of course he could, she realized. Zee bent her head and stirred her Krakatoa Mocha, willing her mind to go smooth and blank.

Catching another person's intent was hard even for an empath trained many years beyond Zee's level. The body had no reason to lie and gave its secrets up easily. But the heart and mind had endless secrets and endless defenses, which very few empaths were ever able to penetrate. She tried anyway, careful to keep her own defenses up. Not just once as they sat in the café but several times. And each time the result was the same. It wasn't that she picked up nothing at all. It was that she could go only so far and then was flung back, forcefully and purposefully. The second time the push-back happened, the words *for your own good* floated in her mind.

She gave him a long, hard look. "What's your real name? On planet Omura, I mean. I don't think it's David Sutton."

"My name is always David Sutton on Earth," he answered, then fell silent.

Yet Zee found it impossible to believe he meant her

harm. Sitting with him, she'd felt protected, as if his long legs were a drawbridge that created a small space just for them. His legs were so close to hers she could feel the warmth of his body. It was like sitting near a low, comforting fire.

Halfway through her Krakatoa Mocha, she asked him how he'd come to be in her A&E room in the first place.

"You have to promise not to laugh," he answered. "I was knocked out. By Nancy Drew. In the stacks at the library. An entire shelf of her fell on me. The originals, not the digitals."

Zee couldn't help it. She laughed. He smiled too and brushed back a cowlick of dark hair. "Do you know how many Nancy Drew books there are? Over a thousand! I was practically buried alive."

"And that's what you're here studying? The literature you came half a galaxy for? I read Nancy Drew when I was ten."

"So did almost every Earth girl for the last three hundred years. It's what you've all got in common." He leaned forward and lowered his voice. "We think Nancy Drew may be the key to female dynamism in the universe."

This time they both laughed.

Zee found the tab on the duvet and reset it to let it

float down onto her shoulders and body. That was what she wanted, that feeling of lightness and warmth near her, the feeling of being in the booth with David again. She wanted to make the feeling last. Because at the end, she'd felt an almost physical snap when he stood, breaking their connection. He hadn't said anything about seeing her again, he hadn't even walked her home. He'd said good-bye outside the café and vanished into the blur of London.

Zee slept most of the day and the next morning put her name on the emergency availability list. She wasn't due back at work until Tuesday, but she didn't want to give herself more time to think about David, either. No one had called in sick, and she'd all but decided to go for a run when suddenly her phone shrieked and all of her screens started to flash. The wall screen shimmered to life and began to feed her information. There'd been another anarchist attack, a shock bomb in Trafalgar Square, and the TBDs were being brought directly to Royal London Hospital.

A swift pulse of adrenalin flooded her veins. Zee had her headset and track shoes on and was flying out the door before the hospital broadcasting system finished ticking through the details.

The bombs had gone off fifteen minutes earlier, one near Nelson's Column and the other across the square by the National Gallery. Nineteen dead at the scene. Twenty-four known injured, 4,654 TBDs.

That was the thing about low-grade shock bombs. They didn't make noise or send up flames and smoke. Instead, an undetectable device the size of a dewdrop, activated by remote control, sent shock waves skipping silently across a large area. The waves weren't strong enough to break glass or bring down buildings. Usually, they didn't even tear the skin. Instead, they passed through the skin to bruise, compress, and tear at soft internal organs.

No one knew who'd been hit and who hadn't, not even the victims. Only a few died right away, usually children and the elderly. Most people insisted they felt fine, unaware of internal injuries that would kill them hours or weeks later, when damaged organs failed or tiny ruptures became infected. Hospital slang classified them as TBDs, patients to be diagnosed. In the three years since the first shock bomb went off in the middle of Paris, not a single bomb had been stopped and not a single bomber had been caught. Those responsible, a group of anarchists who demanded nothing short of a full return to nature and demolition of all cities and social structures, had no support and almost no money, yet they'd mastered a terrifying technology that killed thousands and overwhelmed hospitals wherever they struck. Taking down hospitals was important to the anarchists, who argued that man interfered with natural selection, putting human survival ahead of other animals. "Only when balance is restored can Earth be free" was one of the anarchists' many mottoes.

Zee reached the casualty entrance with the first wave of ambulances. This was the second shock bomb attack she'd worked, and she knew the drill. First hurry to suit up, then attach the sensors to the shaved spots high on the nape of her neck, make sure her hair covered them, and check the master screen to make sure she was logged in and her brain waves were registering.

Hospitals were still developing protocols to deal with shock bombs, and so far empaths were the most promising. Not only were there not enough thermal scanners to handle the high volume of patients, the scanners were incapable of picking up the pinprick damage that could trigger a long, slow death. Empaths had so far been more accurate at triaging patients, separating those who needed immediate care from those who did not. The sensors attached to Zee's skull would monitor her brain activity over the next several hours. Ultimately, it would be mapped and translated into patterns and thoughts that would supply researchers with a far better idea than Zee herself could have given of the hundreds of unvoiced factors that ended in a decision. The final result, researchers hoped, would help train others throughout the world.

The casualty floor was chaos. Because there weren't enough ambulances to handle the flow, hundreds of TBDs came in on their own, while hundreds more were brought by citizens who'd turned out to help. The room was already overflowing, spilling into corridors and leaving a huge crowd outside. Zee saw they were going to have the same problem as last time—telling the TBDs from everyone else. Then she saw Rani swing through the doors with boxes of red, blue, and green glo-markers. She put several of each in Zee's pocket.

"Mark on the forehead," she said, handing out pens to every empath she could reach. "Green for the helper, red for TBDs who need to be seen immediately, one blue line for nonurgent TBDs, and two blue lines for anyone who can wait longer."

"They'll resist," Zee warned, remembering last time, when TBDs went into denial and ripped off the colored paper armbands they'd used.

"Do it fast," Rani advised, "and tell them it will wash off."

"Will it?"

"In about two weeks." Rani grinned and vanished into the crowd.

Zee spent the next hours under combat conditions. There was no quiet place to be, no way to calm patients who were in shock, who convinced themselves that they were fine and could go home and block out everything that had happened. Children were the easiest to work with, especially when she told them she was going to draw a glowing red or blue star on their foreheads. But adults resisted, their bodies hard with fear and closed to her.

She triaged patients as fast as she could, suppressing the constant worry that she was making bad decisions, missing things that could cost someone's life. All the empaths had come in for the emergency, and most of them probably felt the same way she did. Zee saw the head of the department and almost all the teaching and training staff in the crowd. Once, as she hesitated over a diagnosis, her adviser came up to her and pulled her gently aside. "I know it's hard," she said. "But you can't let the fear win, Zee. Right now this is our best option and all of your decisions, even mistakes, help us learn. Do you understand?"

Zee nodded and tried to hold this thought close while she worked. And as the hours went by, she did begin to feel more confident. Tiny signs and patterns revealed themselves to her, and she incorporated them in her decisions. By late afternoon, she was able to clear twice as many patients an hour as she had at first. But no matter how many they processed, there were always more.

She'd just sent a middle-aged man to critical care and was wondering if she could leave the floor long enough to find some juice to drink when she felt a sudden jolt of recognition. David Sutton was in the room, pushing his way through the crowd and coming straight toward her. He carried a child, a girl of about ten, who seemed to be fading in and out of consciousness. When he reached Zee, he held the girl out and said, "This one."

Zee didn't need her empath skills to make the diagnosis. The girl was ashen and had the peculiar, sinking look of someone who was bleeding internally. She looked around the room. There were no available hospital trolleys, but she was able to grab one of the doctors, who found a wheelchair and took her to surgery himself. When she turned to David, his eyes were pleading.

"There are more," he said, motioning to the human pool beyond the casualty doors. "A whole busload of children. The driver died at the wheel, and they crashed."

"All injured?"

"I can't tell for certain, but I'd say most of them."

"Bend down a little." Zee drew a swift green line on his forehead with the glo-marker, then unpinned her own Emergency Worker Priority 1 badge and clipped it to his shirt. "That will get you in and out. Find anyone you can to help you get them in here as fast as you can."

She found the head casualty nurse and explained the situation to her, and by the time David and the volunteers he'd found started bringing them in, Zee had a special station set up in one of the exam rooms. Someone had miraculously found a trolley, and two casualty nurses stood by, ready to administer first aid.

Over the next two hours, they got all thirty-three children off the bus and referred for treatment or release. David slid easily into step beside her and seemed to anticipate what she needed without being told. The smoothness of the way they worked together, fitted together in the cramped space, gave Zee a sense of calm well-being. In a way she couldn't have explained, she felt stronger standing beside him.

By the time they sent the last child off to have a broken arm set and gave up their space in the exam room, it was almost night. Casualty was still crowded, but there was no longer a crowd waiting outdoors, and most of the outdoor triage stations had been dismantled. For the first time, there seemed to be enough staff to handle the flow, and Zee noticed that most of the volunteers had been sent home.

"I guess I should be going too," David said.

After the closeness she'd felt working beside him, Zee felt suddenly awkward. She reminded herself that he could have asked for her phone or her email after breakfast yesterday morning, or even mentioned getting together again, but he hadn't. And now he was going to go again. Chance had brought them together twice, but it was only chance. She didn't want to be one of those girls who convinced herself there was something going on when there wasn't.

"Thank you," she said. "You were great with those kids." She wanted to touch him, to reach up and smooth the twist of hair that sprang away from his forehead like a question mark, to lean forward and rest her forehead against the pulse at the base of his throat. He was beautiful. How could it be that she would never see him again? "Really, I feel like you should get a special commendation or something." She tried to smile. "I mean, it isn't even your planet and—"

"Stop it."

"What?"

He was looking at her intently now, staring straight

into her eyes. "Is there someplace we can go for a minute? Someplace without all these people?"

Something had changed. As discreetly as possible, she pulled the two small sensors from the nape of her neck and slid them into her pocket. Then without a word she led him to the only place she could think of, a tiny supply closet. There was barely enough room for them to stand.

"Anyone would have helped with those kids," he said. "And they weren't even the real reason I came. It was you. I had to make sure you were okay."

Tentatively, as if he weren't sure it was what she wanted, he gathered her to him. Zee felt his arms go around her and felt the warmth of his back and shoulders under her own palms. For a long, delicious moment she let herself lean into him. Then she pulled back.

"Then why did you just vanish yesterday?"

"Because this isn't so good for you. Seeing an alien. Especially now, after the attack. It's only a matter of time before someone blames us for the shock bomb."

"But you were here helping."

"Maybe I was here watching, looking for weak spots in your defenses."

Zee felt a shiver go up her spine. "That's not possible."

"Of course it's possible. And that's what some people will believe." They stood for a long time, wrapped in each other's arms, listening to each other's heart beat. After a while, Zee realized their hearts had found each other's rhythm and were beating in unison.

"What happens now?" David finally asked. "With the anarchists?"

"More shock bombs," Zee said. "That's the usual pattern. They want to make sure we know it's not over. Each time they'll wait just long enough, until we start to feel safe again, until people start to shop, ride the Tube, visit museums, all the things they used to do. Then there'll be another bomb."

"How many?"

"Last time there were five."

He was quiet for a long time before he said, "I should go now. Really." But he kept holding her.

"I want to see you again, David."

She felt his chest expand, then contract with a slow sigh. "I want to see you again too, Zee. But it's too dangerous for you."

She surprised them both by laughing.

"What's so funny?" he asked.

"We just worked a shock bomb cleanup together. We live in a city that's in for months of threats and alerts and more bombings. How many people died today?

Are going to die? And you think *you* are the Big Be Afraid in my life?" She laid her cheek against his chest. "Nothing is safe," she said. "Nothing and no one."

Later, she lingered by the casualty doors as he left. Day had settled into night, and there were still small clusters of people in the ambulance bay. Zee watched until he was lost in the security queue stretching from the Whitechapel Tube station checkpoint.

This time, she knew, he wouldn't vanish.

CHAPTER FIVE

THE GIRL WITH WATERFALL HAIR

*Z*ee had forgotten all the things that came in the wake of a shock bomb—the worried calls from her parents and emails from Jasmine asking if she and Rani were all right, the empty streets that took twice as long to navigate because of all the security checkpoints, the slow work of matching unidentified victims with missing persons reports.

London was all but cut off as anti-anarchist forces searched for anyone who might be connected to the attack. Only a few Tube lines were running, and the vactrains, the trains that flew through vacuum tunnels beneath the old BritRail tracks, had been shut down, as had the airports. There was no public transport in or out of London, and making it past the checkpoints in a private car required a pass. People kept showing up at the hospital, convinced they'd been in the blast range when mostly they were just lonely and frightened. They all needed to be screened and diagnosed, and over the next few days, Zee worked until she swayed on her feet with exhaustion. Other than a few hours snatched here and there, she didn't get another real day off for almost two weeks, and the week after that, when the vactrains were running again, she and David had their first date.

They hadn't had much time to talk since the shock bomb, and the thread of magic they'd found in the supply closet began to seem a bit unreal. After all, David was older than she was, and had just turned nineteen. For all she knew, she might be just one of many girls in his world. Worlds, to be accurate. He might have someone waiting for him on his planet, Omura. To him, Zee might be like the sweets you ate on holiday, something that didn't really count.

Even so, she was looking forward to seeing him again. "I want to do something fun," he'd told her. "Not productive or useful or educational. Just fun."

Fun was in short supply on results-oriented Omura, he'd explained. People stayed fit by completing two short, highly effective workouts a day. They ate food manufactured for nutrition, and all their music was educational, featuring lyrics that helped people remember the bones of the body or math formulas. In their free time, they formed teams and held contests to see who could pick up the most litter or submit the best solution for a traffic flow problem.

"You mean you don't do anything just for fun? You don't go barefoot in wet grass? Or do things that make you feel like the world is bigger and more interesting than you thought it was? Like travel?"

"There's no reason to travel anymore. The CGA, our Central Governing Authority, stabilized the planet several hundred years ago. The climate is pleasant and uniform from pole to pole. Everyone speaks the same language and has the same goals. There's nothing you can get in one place on Omura that you can't get everywhere else. This frees us to carry forward our technology and our research. It's why we're so far ahead of you, even though intelligent life began in both places about the same time."

"Then why—"

"Why are we here studying your arts and music? Even Nancy Drew and nail polish colors? Because in some way we can't understand, all this inefficiency seems to make you more efficient at the one thing that truly matters."

"What's that?"

"Surviving. Our population is shrinking. No one's interested in having children. Or anything, really. By eliminating inefficiency, we've made true equality possible. Everyone on the planet has the same resources and options. No one goes without food or fuel. We're freer than ever to carry our research and technology forward, but no one seems to care. The more inefficiency we eliminate, the fewer new ideas we get. And when setbacks occur, instead of solving the problem, teams scrap the project and refuse to work on it again. Somehow, all your inefficiencies make you want to live, and wanting to live gives you new ideas."

"But you're not like that," Zee had protested.

"No, that's why I'm here. Hundreds of thousands of years ago, Omura took the wrong evolutionary turn. And now, rather than die out, we're trying to learn. So help me with the experiment. Let's do something that's just for fun."

Zee thought for a moment. "I know just the thing."

"What is it?"

"Oh, no, I'm not telling—you have to learn to be

surprised and take things as they come," she'd told him. "That's part of the deal. Meet me at Victoria Station Saturday morning at ten by the Southern Line ticket booth."

What Zee hadn't anticipated were the crowds. After being trapped in London for a few weeks, people were eager to get away. The vactrain to Brighton took less than fifteen minutes, but the queue was the longest she'd ever seen. Zee had begun to wonder how she and David would find each other when she saw him in the crowd. He seemed to be talking to a tall girl with a waterfall of shining black hair, but as Zee approached, she was relieved to see the girl nudge the young man beside her and disappear with him into the crowd. Zee felt a surge of relief. Even without seeing the girl's face, Zee knew she was beautiful.

"Is this what you meant by taking things as they come?" David asked lightly. "A lesson in crowd tolerance?"

"Sorry about that. Let's hope the queue moves fast and they've put extra trains on."

"It's okay." He smiled. "I can't think of anyone I'd rather be in line with." He put his hand lightly on her back to draw her closer to him, and she knew that her fears about awkward moments were unfounded.

It was Zee who came up with the idea of imagining how every couple in line had met, but David who said they should also predict their future. Zee did the first three couples, coming up with meetings that made David laugh. He got into the spirit and told her the wealthy looking retired couple had met years ago when the husband was a burglar and the wife, a police officer, arrested him and inspired him to go straight. He said she'd been on the lookout for a good-looking thief to reform for some time.

Zee told the story of how her parents had met, which David found fascinating. "Is that something that runs in families?" he wanted to know. "Are you an early decider too?"

"I don't know. I've never decided before," she answered, and David took her hand.

Zee didn't even notice how they'd moved up in the queue until she realized the crowd in front of them was so small they were sure to get on the next train. Then she noticed—that one couple up ahead was the girl with ink black hair, the one she'd thought David had spoken to earlier. Now that she could see her face, Zee realized she'd been right in thinking the girl was beautiful. She was tall, with high, broad cheekbones that made her face almost round. Yet there was something willowy and delicate and confident about her.

Zee nudged David. "Your turn," she said.

David followed her gaze, and Zee was sure she saw a look of recognition. He held his hands up in surrender. "I'm out of stories, Zee. You win. Besides, it's almost our turn to board."

She gazed at him firmly. "Do you know that girl?"

"What girl?" he asked in a way that made Zee realize he absolutely *did* know her. Confused, she decided to forget the girl for now and not let her day be ruined.

The sun was high when they got out at Brighton and were plunged instantly into the bright, swirling throng. Zee fought against the crowd to keep them from being pulled toward the beach.

"Aren't we going to the pier?" David asked.

"Not yet," Zee said. She felt excited, and when they finally struggled free of the masses, she led them quickly inland, past the food stalls and the shops, until they arrived at what looked like a vast green meadow. Above the meadow, people balanced on surfboards and coasted ten or twenty feet in the air. Some seemed to glide up a curving wall, do a complete loop, and go on their way. Others lost their balance and fell onto the green of the meadow, which turned out to be as soft and yielding as marshmallows, swallowing them up for a few seconds, then popping them back to the surface, where they would reclaim their boards, lie flat on their stomachs, appear to touch the board in a certain place, and rise slowly into the air. Then they would get to their feet and go shooting off through the air as if nothing had ever happened.

"I hope you're up for this," Zee said, her cheeks flushed with excitement. "I haven't been airboarding for years, but I used to love it. My dad taught me."

They checked their belongings and rented boards. Zee showed David how to read the symbol-coded signs around the park. Beginners' air currents were in the front, nearest the sea. The farther from the sea you went, the stronger the currents became.

Zee pointed out an area far from them, at the very back, where the green foam of the meadow was marked with black diamonds. "Don't go there unless you want to get rag dolled. Wicked air."

She showed him the pressure points built into the board and how to get the board aloft and stand on it. He wiped out twice before he could do it, but laughed each time and tried again. He was, she saw, a quick learner, and within an hour, they were riding the advanced beginners' waves together. They tried riding in together holding hands but tumbled off their boards each time, falling together into the softness of the meadow. Neither of them seemed to mind, and neither was quick to let go of the other's hand.

By the time they turned in their boards, they were tired and breathless and leaning on each other.

"That was great," David said, slinging his arm around her. "And now I'm so hungry I could eat a horse."

The sun was starting to dip, and they headed for the pier. There were all sorts of shops along the way, old-fashioned shops that sold things no one needed but everyone seemed to want. Candles. Charms. Books printed on paper. Clothes that had gone out of style a hundred years ago. Buttons with pictures of all three Queen Elizabeths on them, sixteenth century, twentieth century, and the one on the throne now. Some poses were serious; others showed them with pink glitter crowns on their heads.

"Why do people buy all this stuff?" David asked.

Zee shrugged. "For a bit of a laugh, I guess. For fun. To take home to friends as gifts and make them feel remembered."

"That's crazy," David said.

They walked on and, while Zee was gazing at a window that contained a complete and highly detailed replica of Buckingham Palace in chocolate, David suddenly broke away from her, promising to be back in a minute. Zee watched him disappear into Ye Olde Book Shoppe, glad he'd left her in front of the chocolate shop. They'd talked about books before, and it was as if they'd been speaking different languages. David genuinely loved books and said there was no greater pleasure than holding an old-style printed book in your hands, but she'd read very few of the things he had. Empaths were discouraged from reading, she explained, because the thoughts and feelings in books could seep into their minds and interfere with their perceptions. The conversation had left Zee feeling sad and a little jealous of the books he was so passionate about.

When he came out of the shop, he was carrying a small square tied in paper with a sea-colored silk ribbon. "This is for you," he said. "For today."

She didn't want to open it. Not right away. She wanted to have the little package with the blue ribbon to look forward to, so the day wouldn't be over. David seemed to read her thoughts and smiled. "It's for you to open at home. Right now, I'm starved. Let's get some fish and chips."

Later they both knew it was time to head back, but found one excuse after another to stay just a little longer. David kept glancing at his watch, as if portioning out the time. The last thing they did was stroll along the beach. It wasn't really dark, with so many lights from the pier and the shops, and it certainly wasn't private. But it felt both dark and private when he put his arms around her and kissed her.

It was the first *real* kiss of Zee's life, and it felt like a current of mercury gliding through her body, smooth and silver and full of a sweet, heavy weight all its own. After all the years of feeling immune, of being convinced this drawing, drowning feeling would never happen to her, she realized it *was* happening, had happened, and would never *un*happen. Without a moment's hesitation, she kissed him back, hoping she was kissing him the same way he'd kissed her, making him feel the delicious slow sliding of magic though his bones, but not knowing, because it was something she'd never done before.

"I wish . . . ," he said after a while, "I wish things were different, Zee."

"So do I," she said. "I wish I had an apartment we could go back to. We can't have visitors at Ford Square."

"Zee . . ."

"But you have an apartment," she whispered. "My day off lasts until tomorrow night. I don't have to go back to the residence hall. If I call Rani, she'll cover for me. Rani is great at things like that."

David was gently disentangling the two of them. "I can't, Zee. *We* can't."

"Why not?"

"It's too complicated to explain. And you wouldn't like the answer. I'm sorry."

Suddenly, she felt horribly embarrassed. Worse, she felt a tear spill down her cheek. He must have seen it in the moonlight, because he checked it with his thumb and kissed the top of her head.

"It's not you, Zee. It's nothing to do with you."

"Then tell me."

"I can't."

It didn't help that on the vactrain going home she again saw the girl with the waterfall of black hair or that once again she imagined seeing a glance of recognition pass between the girl and David.

CHAPTER SIX

SECOND WAVE

The minute Mrs. Hart opened the door, Zee felt brightness. It wasn't just the elegant bracelet of Neptune's Tears that sparkled on her wrist. It was something that streamed through the open door, as if the air inside were lighter than the air outside. To Zee, the sparkle of the Neptune's Tears always mirrored Mrs. Hart's vibrant spirit.

"Come in, Zee, dear. It's so good to see you again."

There was no way Mrs. Hart could possibly know how glad Zee was to be there at all. For almost a week she'd been on pins and needles, not knowing whether she'd be allowed to come or not. Mrs. Hart had specifically asked for Zee to work with her at home during this last phase of her illness. A significant honor to come so early in an empath's career, her adviser pointed out, but also a significant responsibility. It was more than a question of helping patients with physical pain; it was helping them meet the end of life, a task that required not only skill and rapport with the patient but the maturity to sublimate all one's own beliefs to the beliefs of the patient. Empaths often heard things—anger and grievances, confessions and guilts—that the patient could tell no one else. The empath's natural tendency was to ease the patient's way by trying to fix the situation or urging the patient to a different point of view. But this was exactly what the empath must not do. As Zee's adviser put it, "This is one river you must let flow by itself and find its own way to the sea."

Zee's youth and inexperience alone were cause for concern, but there was also the matter of the patient known as David Sutton. Zee had lost the barrier between self and empath and failed to connect with—or help—the patient. Zee's adviser read Zee's report of the incident. Zee had decided not to mention seeing David on her own time unless she absolutely had to, but she did point out that he had helped as a volunteer after the shock bomb and that the two of them had worked effectively together, hoping this would lessen the importance of her initial failure.

"Yes, we were told about his assistance with the shock bomb victims."

Zee was caught by surprise. She knew it hadn't come from Rani, who'd spent most of that frantic afternoon helping triage patients in the parking lot. "Who—?"

"We were also told that David Sutton wasn't supposed to be your patient, that you'd prepped for another case and were switched without time to prepare. Is that right?"

Zee nodded. Piper! She had to be the source for both stories. But what was in it for Piper? Zee was so baffled she almost missed hearing her adviser say that in view of her overall excellent record and Mrs. Hart's insistence, the request was approved. The next time Zee saw Piper, she thanked her.

"I never meant for anything to happen. I was just . . ." Piper paused, as if choosing her words carefully. "Just tired of you being everyone's golden girl. I just wanted to take your leg bud patient and rattle you. A mild piercing, that was all. I didn't mean for anything else to happen." Her voice faded to a whisper. "After all, if anyone knows how distracting love can be, it's me."

This was how Zee knew her secret wasn't exactly a secret anymore. Piper had seen the truth of David's effect on her. And, for some reason, taken pity.

❧ ⋆ ⋆

On the outside, Mrs. Hart's house looked very much like all the other Hampstead Terrace houses. Inside, it was very much like Mrs. Hart, elegant and irreverent. The walls were a soft butternut color, with white wood-work and crown moldings. Against this were bright splashes: a pillow the color of peacock feathers, a chair in bright red silk, a bowl of clear green glass whose rippling edges were like an ocean wave. Zee had never been in a room quite like it, yet she felt instantly at home.

"I brought some reading material from the hospital," she began, suddenly feeling the weight of her task. "Different experts suggest different approaches." Zee laid the loaded reader on the coffee table.

Mrs. Hart set it aside. "Oh, experts! I don't think we'll need those. I'm not much for experts! I did have some pain the other night, and I'd rather not take the pills. Why don't we just talk about some things I can do for it. And I could use advice about talking to my daughters. The younger one especially, who just turned seventy, seems to feel I can live forever if I just put my mind to it. How can I tell her I don't *want* to put my mind to it? Wouldn't do it if I could. I've had a good life, and I'm tired. I want to see John again." Her eyes flicked toward a photo, the old-fashioned flat kind, not a hologram.

"Your husband?" Zee asked, following her glance. "Wow, he was gorgeous."

"You better believe it. And now I want to see him again. You see, I've been without him all these years, and I'm tired of waiting. I don't exactly know what comes next, but I know John will be there." She fell silent for a moment. "Someone once said, 'Life is either a daring adventure or nothing.' I guess that's true of death too."

A shiver went up Zee's spine. She had heard the same quote for the very first time just the other day, from David. "Helen Keller."

"What, dear?"

"Helen Keller said that. She lived about two hundred years ago. She was blind and deaf and—"

"I know who Helen Keller is, dear. I'm glad you do too. Well, let's get started. Do you have some suggestions for me? My daughter really can be exhausting, and takes on so."

When she'd first sat down, Zee had felt a moment

of panic, overwhelmed by the situation. But Mrs. Hart's questions were focused and somehow ordinary. Over the next hour, Zee explained various ways of meeting the pain and helped Mrs. Hart develop several personalized exercises. They discussed Mrs. Hart's daughter as well, Zee listening more than talking and feeling they'd made progress when Mrs. Hart concluded that she needed to give her daughter time to accept things in her own way.

"That's all I can manage for today," the older woman said suddenly. "But I hope you don't have to go rushing off. I'd love a cup of tea and a chat, and maybe we can make a dent in the pastries people keep bringing me."

Zee was halfway through her lemon curd tart when Mrs. Hart surprised her by asking, "Now, if it isn't prying, what's troubling my favorite empath?"

Zee finished chewing and swallowed. "Does it show?"

Mrs. Hart said nothing, waiting for Zee to go on, but Zee remained quiet. "Ah. Silence. That usually means a man."

"Mrs. Hart—"

"Ellie. We can't be having a cozy chat if you're still calling me Mrs. Hart."

"Ellie. I'm not sure I should go into it all. I'm supposed to be here helping you with pain management techniques."

"No, you're supposed to be helping me manage pain effectively. Nothing would be a more effective distraction than hearing someone else's troubles for a change. Although I respect your privacy."

The truth was, Zee was dying to talk about David. So far she'd told no one, not even Rani or Jasmine, about him. So the whole story tumbled out to a rapt audience of one. She told Mrs. Hart how they'd met, how he'd taken her to breakfast, and how, despite his being an alien, she'd found herself thinking about him over and over again. And she talked about the confusion as well, about how she was always aware that there was something he wasn't telling her, and little things he told her that didn't quite match up, and how she sometimes wondered if she was wrong to trust him.

"And you really like him?" Mrs. Hart asked thoughtfully. "You really think he's someone who could be important in your life?" Zee nodded. "Then there's only one question that matters. Is he a good person? Do you think he has a good heart?"

"Yes." Zee thought of the times she'd felt connected to him and the times she'd felt pushed back. Even then, she'd always felt he was pushing her away to protect her from something. "Yes, he has a good heart."

"Because people can seem to do the right thing, the thing you want, but do it for selfish reasons. And people who care about you can do things you find confusing. But if I had to pick, I'd pick the person with the good heart. How long did you say you've known him?"

"Almost two months."

Mrs. Hart laughed. "Oh, my, two whole months. And you don't know every single thing about him! Yes, no wonder you're frustrated." She laughed again. "Two months out of what could be a lifetime! Oh, Zee, if you knew everything about him now, what would you do for the next one hundred years? No one can tell you who they are—they *show* you who they are, and that takes time."

As Zee had predicted to David, the Trafalgar Square shock bomb was followed by a second attack, two months later. On the last Sunday of August, the anarchists struck again.

Zee was with a patient when a sudden, piercing pain spiked through her head so forcefully she bent double. Grateful that her patient—a post-op stroke victim whose damaged brain had been spliced and patched with a regrown section—was still under anesthesia, she managed to find the call button, then stumbled to a chair. She felt as if she might be going blind, but when she covered first one eye, then the other, she found that the uncovered eye could see normally each time. Her jaw was clenched, and waves of nausea seemed to begin in her head and sweep though her body. She knew this wasn't logical and wondered if she was having a stroke or a seizure. Worse was what she described later as the silent scream. She knew she wasn't hearing real screaming but felt it in her head, hundreds and hundreds of people, their voices knit in an endless cry of horror. By the time an orderly reached her, she was exhausted with fear and barely felt herself being helped onto a gurney.

Waking up, she knew from the slant of light in the room it was early evening. Two familiar faces, Rani's and her adviser's, were looking down at her.

"What happened to me?"

The room was tranquil and smelled faintly of oranges. The silent screaming that had filled her head was gone. The pain was gone too. Zee moved her hand and noticed a blood pressure thimble on the tip of her index finger. She was wearing a hospital gown, and a gauze pad was taped to the crook of her elbow. They'd drawn blood. Slowly, she reached her other hand up and felt the EEG leads attached to her temples, to her forehead, just behind her ears, and at the base of her skull.

For once, there was no mischief in Rani's eyes. Her adviser had no expression at all.

"What happened to me?" she asked again.

CHAPTER SEVEN

ONE RAINDROP

Zee was clearly waiting for an answer.

The adviser turned her head slightly. "Rani."

Rani stepped close to the bed and gave Zee a quick hug. "Don't be afraid, Zee," she whispered. "You're the one raindrop. I'll see you in the morning."

After she left, Zee's adviser stepped into her place. "First," she said, "there's nothing physically wrong with you. We'll have the EEG analyzed in detail, but Dr. Branning and I both think it looks fine."

Zee realized there was a third person in the room, sitting off to the side. He rose at the mention of his name. "We haven't met before, I don't think. I'm with the psych department. Separate building."

Psych department?

"Is there something wrong?" Zee asked. "With my brain? Did I—I don't remember too well—did I *do* something?" A horrible possibility flashed through her mind. "Did I hurt a patient?"

"No, no, nothing like that," her adviser assured her. "We're quite sure we have the answer. But Dr. Branning has some questions to ask."

A wave of exhaustion washed over her. "Could we do it tomorrow? When I'm fresh? I'm just so tired right now."

Dr. Branning had a kind smile. "I'm sorry, Zee, but we really need to do this now, when you're stale."

That made her smile. "Okay," she said. "Shoot."

For the next half hour, Zee answered the oddest assortment of questions she'd ever been asked. Was there a radio on in the room she'd had the attack in? Or anywhere nearby? Was she aware of any significant news stories? When was the last time she'd seen a news screen? Been online? Did she dream often? What about? What was the last dream she remembered? Had anyone told her their dreams lately? Yes? What were they? What images and techniques had she used with her most recent patients? What did she and Mrs. Hart discuss in their sessions? What was the last hologram she'd watched? Was she reading any books just now? No? When was the last time she'd read a book, and what was it about? When had she had her last period? What were her periods usually like? Were they accompanied by dizziness? Visual or auditory hallucinations? Did she ever think she heard voices? Did she know today's date? The prime minister's name? Her own name and address?

By the time Dr. Branning finished, Zee could barely keep her eyes open. And even with her eyes closed, she knew her adviser and Dr. Branning were conferring about her in lowered voices. She no longer cared. She just wanted to be left alone, or have Rani come back. Instead, she opened her eyes to find Dr. Branning staring down at her.

"Ah, good." He drew up a chair. "What happened to you is quite rare, but not abnormal. My specialty is mass psychology, in particular a branch called noetics. The idea that thoughts have substance and can be picked up by others isn't new, but it wasn't until about two hundred years ago that we had proof."

He paused to make sure he had Zee's attention. "Researchers back then discovered that whenever a fresh puzzle was published—be it crossword or jigsaw or any other type of puzzle—the first people who solved it took the longest. But the more often the puzzle was solved, the more quickly others solved it, even though each person worked on their own, in isolation. The answers, you see, were out there, thoughts in the air, picked up and used by others. For the most part, this activity goes on undetected, in the subconscious. People aren't aware that they've tapped into the thought swarm, even when the thoughts are disturbing."

Again, Dr. Branning paused to make sure Zee was following him. "About the same time the puzzle data surfaced, researchers at Princeton University were monitoring patterns of mass consciousness. There was a severe, widespread disturbance in the group pattern in the days before 9/11, yet no one predicted the event beforehand. The subconscious, by and large, defends its secrets. The conscious can bang at the gates all it wants, but the road remains closed, often for the overall good of the organism. There are rare cases, however, when someone possesses or develops a mind in perfect unity, where the subconscious passes along information it deems vital. That person is the one in ten million, the single raindrop that fills the ocean. The transmission, of course, is imperfect, for the conscious mind communicates in words while the language of the subconscious is images and feelings, sometimes elements as elusive as touch and scent."

At this point, Zee's adviser came forward. "We're sorry about all the tests, Zee, and drawing blood, but we had to eliminate all other possibilities. Now we have, and we're certain that's what happened to you today. You see, at exactly the time you had your, uh, episode, shock bombs went off in Dublin, Gdansk, Shanghai, Houston, and Toronto."

"*What*? You're telling me I *knew* about the bombs?"

"No. You caught the thoughts of those who were there, and those thoughts manifested themselves in you as physical symptoms."

Zee's hand felt ice cold on the bed's guardrail. That storm of silent screams! The fire-hot pain at the base of her skull! The realization that she'd caught the final thoughts of hundreds of dead people spiraled into a tidal wave of nausea. Be calm, she told herself. Focus. Stay logical. She took a deep breath.

"Okay. What do we do now? How do I stop this?"

"That's the thing," her adviser said. "There's no real way to stop these incidents. In fact, each time this happens makes it more likely to happen again. The body learns from itself."

"But I can't live with this," Zee protested. "It's

too . . . too . . . big." Her voice saying *big* sounded pathetically small. Neither of the faces gazing down at her looked surprised at her alarm. A sudden thought struck her. "Is this because I'm an empath?"

"Not directly, no."

"Not *directly*? What's *that* supposed to mean?"

"This isn't the result of being an empath. Your training didn't create this. But the traits that make you a good empath also make you a good receptor. And both your training and your work made it more likely to happen."

Zee was suddenly furious. "Why didn't you tell us this was a possibility when we were in training? Didn't you think we had a right to know?"

"In the early days of empathy, we did," Dr. Banning said. "I developed the protocol. But we discovered it triggers false episodes in a large number of trainees. We never saw a real case. Apparently because the phenomenon is rare."

Zee studied their faces. "What do I do now?"

"There are three possible paths," her adviser explained. "First, you could give up being an empath. It wouldn't guarantee anything, but it *would* decrease the odds of this happening again."

"Or?"

"Or you could continue as an empath and cope with the occasional episode. There's no medication for this, but there are strategies, blunting techniques that would help block both the physical and emotional pain."

"And the third path?"

"You could accept it," Dr. Branning said. "You could develop your talent and take control of it, own it. You could become a diviner."

Zee crossed her arms, a gesture of childish sullenness she hadn't indulged in for years. "Why would I want to do that?"

"Because you're the one in ten million. The raindrop that fills the ocean."

"No thanks."

"But you could do a great deal of good, Zee."

"Frederick!" Zee's adviser hissed. "She's had enough for one day."

But Dr. Branning would not be stopped. "A great deal of good in the world. Finding the missing. Harvesting the last thoughts of the dead at crime scenes. Even forestalling attacks like the ones today. Of course, it takes a good deal of training and total commitment, but—"

"Frederick!" The adviser looked daggers at Dr. Branning. "Please go now."

Zee waited until she heard the soft click of the door closing. "Is that true?" she asked. "Are there people like me who could have stopped those bombings today? Could *I* have stopped those bombings today?"

"It isn't that simple, Zee."

"Could I?" Her adviser kept silent. "Please say."

"Yes. Yes, I believe you could do that. In time. But the price can be high. It isn't always an easy life."

"Have you known a diviner?"

"Yes. Once."

"Where is she now?"

"*He.* A young man I cared for very much. He was captured by the anarchists. Six years of torture does terrible things to a human being. They turned him."

"What was his name?"

"Now he goes by the name of his creation, Thanatos."

Zee gasped. Thanatos was the man-made virus that had killed one in ten children the year Zee was twelve. She still remembered that year of fearfulness and isolation, of being kept at home behind closed doors, of her mother obsessively scrubbing every inch of the house every week, her hands raw from the lye she added to the washing-up water. *Thanatos*, her father told her, was the Greek word for "death."

"He was a good man once," her adviser said gently. "The diviner's way is difficult, Zee. A path that takes more than it gives."

"Do I have to decide right now?"

"Oh, no, love. You don't 'have to' do anything. And don't let Dr. Branning push you into anything, either."

Zee felt bone tired. Three months ago, when she'd met David Sutton, her whole life and much of what she'd believed about herself had changed. Today it had changed again.

"Does anyone know about me?"

"Just Rani. We know she's your best friend here, and we didn't think you should go through this alone."

"Are you going to tell my family?"

"Not unless you want us to."

"*No!* No."

Long after her supervisor had gone, Zee lay alone in the dark as two cold tears trickled down her cheeks. She wanted it to be this morning again. She wanted to be an empath. She wanted to be the girl who worked with Mrs. Hart, who worried about her patients and could spend hours thinking about David Sutton.

She didn't want what had been given to her.

CHAPTER EIGHT

BLACKFRIARS BRIDGE

The next morning, Zee awakened confident and full of calm, focused energy. She rose early, showered, signed out as a patient, and signed back in as an empath. She wanted her stroke victim back, and she meant to get him. Step one was to find Rani and make sure she was willing to transfer the case back, which shouldn't be a problem since Rani had her own heavy caseload and had seen Mr. Caldwell just once, while he was in post-op twilight.

Rani was alone in the empath's lounge, drinking tea and watching her favorite Hindi soap opera. For as long as Zee had known Rani, the soap opera had been exactly the same. It was always about a young girl trying to avoid the marriage her parents had arranged. Sometimes she escaped with the village boy she really loved. Sometimes she didn't escape, but over the next season fell in love with her new husband. Once a girl had thrown herself into the sea but was rescued by a handsome young fisherman who turned out to be a prince.

Usually, nothing could tear Rani away from these tales, but today she blanked the screen the minute she saw Zee, and when Zee explained that she'd like to reclaim Mr. Caldwell, Rani volunteered to immediately resign from the case in writing. Then, not quite looking at Zee, she held up the package she'd been nibbling from. "Ginger cookie? Or can I make you some tea?" Her brow furrowed as if she were trying to tempt an invalid to eat.

Zee understood what was happening. "Oh, no, Kapoor, she said, reverting to their student habit of calling each other by their last names. "Don't tell me you took that divining stuff seriously. That seems to be Dr. Branning's favorite theme. But he got the wrong end of the stick. What happened was a one-off, a fluke."

Rani perked up a little. "Really?"

"Of *course*. Dr. Branning is just so anxious for Royal London to have its very own diviner." Zee shook her head. "That isn't me. I'm not anyone's dewdrop."

"Raindrop," Rani corrected.

"Whatever. Raindrop, dewdrop, lemondrop. Not me."

"Gumdrop?" Rani giggled.

"That either."

By nine A.M. Mr. Caldwell was Zee's patient again. A few days later she had an idea for helping him that might help lots of other patients as well. Mr. Caldwell's speech center had been severely affected. The regrown and patched-in slice of brain, though fully functional, was blank as a baby's and would have to be remapped. From talking to his wife, Zee learned Mr. Caldwell had been an avid gardener and, since he still lacked the coordination needed to navigate a screen, she had made a simple slideshow for him.

"I have a little surprise for you," she said, propping a screen before him and showing him how a single tap would advance the picture. When Zee's pictures of lush garden flowers began their parade in response to his tap, Mr. Caldwell's eyes lit up. As he looked at the picture, she spoke the name of the flower several times, hoping the pictures, the words, and Mr. Caldwell's lifelong enthusiasm would form the foundations of a healing bridge.

"Rose," Zee said when a large pink and cream blossom with abundant petals filled the screen.

But Mr. Caldwell frowned and became agitated, shaking his head *No, no, no*. He held up one forefinger, then held up the other one beside it. When Zee failed to understand, he repeated the gesture. Finally, glancing from Mr. Caldwell to the picture, she understood.

"Two roses?" she asked.

"Dhubba," Mr. Caldwell struggled to say, his brow wrinkling in frustration.

Suddenly, Zee understood. "Double rose? Is that it?"

Exhausted, Mr. Caldwell sank back against his pillows, but Zee could see a faint nod of satisfaction.

"Roadj. Dhubba roadj," Mr. Caldwell said faintly. It was a good start.

***

At first, the multiple bombs seemed to be a major victory for the anarchists. Stock markets fell, people got into arguments and accidents, governments came up with protocols no one could follow. Then something changed. So many people in so many cities had been affected that their thoughts turned and focused on the anarchists like a swarm of angry bees. Ideas, as Dr. Branning might say, were out there. And not all of the ideas were bad. After years of feeling like sitting ducks, people began to see ways of fighting back. A flutist in

Vienna suggested lining public places with exquisitely sensitive tuning forks that would sound an alert if touched by the shock waves.

One of the most successful ideas was the Shock Sock, a microfiber tube that folded into a package smaller than a deck of cards. In case of attack, the user slid the corsetlike tube over his torso so the tube encased the entire trunk of the body. Pulling a ring caused the tube to contract. If the person hadn't been injured, no harm was done, but if he had been hurt, the compression slowed internal bleeding and kept organs functioning for up to forty-eight hours. Factories swung into high gear, and within weeks, governments were distributing them to citizens. Zee's was blue and identified her as a Priority 1 Responder. David's was gray with a red AG for Alien Guest. Zee didn't like to think about the markings, because she knew they meant that in an attack she would be evaluated and treated first, while David would be left to the very end.

In early October, Royal London was asked to contribute to a three-day seminar on shock bomb triage held in Paris. Emergency services, surgery, and the department of empathy were specifically invited. In addition to senior and teaching staff, four teams of three empaths each would train empaths from around the world. The good news was, Zee and Rani both made the cut and were on the same team. The bad news was that their third team member was Piper. Zee spent most of the long weekend on tenter hooks, hoping Piper wouldn't reveal her relationship with David to Rani. On their one free afternoon, Zee and Rani went to the city's colorful and extravagant flea markets. While Rani was trying on her hundredth vintage dress, Zee drifted to a jewelry seller nearby. In a tray of antique charms, she saw a small silver eagle in a circle of silver on a leather thong. David had once said that of all Earth's animals, so different from those on Omura, his favorite was the American eagle. Now that he knew her, he said, he liked the eagle even more. Zee bought the talisman without hesitation, even though it took most of her spending money. She wasn't sure if she was ready to give David such a personal gift, or if he'd remember the comment he made, but she knew the eagle was meant to be his and she needed to buy it.

"That must be for someone special."

Zee whirled around to see Piper standing behind her. Before she could say anything, Piper gave her an unreadable smile and melted back into the crowd. For all Zee's worries, Piper never said a word about David, and at the end of the weekend, even Rani noted that Piper had been almost-not-quite-but-very-close-to normal.

"Maybe she's just vibing the way everyone feels,"

Zee said. That happened with empaths a lot. The skill was always there, on duty or off, and when there was a mass mood afoot, empaths often picked up on it.

"It's possible," Rani said.

Everyone's mood had improved over the last few weeks. Even though the anarchists hadn't been caught and there was still no way to detect a shock bomb before it went off, people no longer felt helpless. They were developing survival strategies. Just as they had eventually found a remedy for the Thanatos virus, they would find a remedy for this, too. They would eventually find a remedy for everything the anarchists tried, and then they would find the anarchists themselves.

***

Zee willingly rearranged her schedule to make home visits to Mrs. Hart on Tuesday and Friday afternoons. Though her adviser was pleased with her performance, Zee sometimes wondered who got more out of their sessions, herself or Mrs. Hart. No one in Zee's world had ever died before, except for a great-great-grandmother she hadn't seen since she was six months old. As Mrs. Hart stepped closer to the end of her life with each visit, Zee saw there was something natural and even freeing about it, and that who you were and how you'd lived came shining through to the very end.

One day she arrived to find Mrs. Hart at an easel, painting.

"I've heard that if there's a skill you're working on near the end, you can pick up where you left off on the other side," she explained. "This is a picture of the house I grew up in. I probably won't live to finish it, but so be it." Mrs. Hart caught Zee blinking rapidly. "Now, now, no tears. We agreed. And I expect they'll find an apprenticeship for me over there somewhere. After all, I'm dying to get in." Mrs. Hart chuckled but stopped when Zee didn't join in. "Really, dear, this isn't such a big deal."

But it was a big deal to Mrs. Hart's daughter, who cried every time she visited and sent far too many email updates on newly discovered miracle cures. Watching her sadness wash over Mrs. Hart, Zee realized that if you truly loved someone, letting go of them was sometimes part of that love. She resolved that when her parents came to the same crossroads, she would put their needs ahead of her own.

Mrs. Hart finished wiping off her brushes. "Now, dear, before we start—and I'll need more help with that pain in my side, it's like being bitten by a wolf—tell me about that boyfriend of yours. What's happening? Did you give him that eagle yet?"

"Not yet," Zee said. "I still don't know how he feels. Not for sure."

Without Mrs. Hart, Zee would have had no one to say this to. She still hadn't told Rani about David because she knew what Rani would say. To Rani, boys were like outfits you took into the dressing room. If one pinched at the waist or didn't make you happy, there were dozens more on the rack.

For Zee, David was the one, but the more she believed that he cared for her, the more she sensed there was something that would forever keep him at a distance. She had told him all about her family, but he had told her nothing about his. He seldom spoke of Omura, and the only details she knew were ones she picked up by asking pointed questions. Did they have pets, or were animals considered frivolous and unproductive? Were the colors the same? How did women wear their hair? Sometimes he gave a vague answer. Sometimes he distracted her with a joke or a kiss. Twice she was sure his answers contradicted things he'd said before.

And then there was the big issue, the one Zee was too embarrassed to talk to Mrs. Hart about, because it would have started with describing that moment in Brighton when Zee had wanted to spend the night with him and he'd turned her down. Her cheeks still burned with the shame of rejection whenever she thought of it.

Zee couldn't help but notice that their dates always began with a meeting in some public place—a park, in front of a theater, the Victoria Embankment. They held hands, walked arm in arm, and kissed like any other couple, and there were times when their desire burned so hot Zee was sure they'd end up in his apartment in a tangle of sheets. But at some point, he'd draw back, and the date would end with him putting her into a taxi and kissing her lightly on the forehead. A few times, when she arrived a few minutes early or the taxi taking her home got a slow start, she thought she saw the young woman with the long black hair, then did her best to convince herself she was mistaken.

Wasn't it funny, Zee often thought to herself, that resolving Mrs. Hart's pain was so much easier than resolving her own?

On a warm November Saturday, they spent the whole day together at the festival that was held each autumn along the Thames, when the whole riverside was turned into an old-style open-air market, with souvenirs, food stalls, street artists, and wandering performers and musicians. David had a stomachache from eating too many apple tarts, and they were resting on a park bench until he got his second wind. Later, after sunset, they planned to cross Blackfriars Bridge, carrying lanterns like everyone else, and find a good spot to watch the grand finale laser show.

"Never let me eat another apple tart," he groaned.

"I don't know," she teased back. "I tried to get between you and that last one, and it was a dangerous place to be."

They watched tides of people stroll by. Some were wearing costumes and masks, and children had their faces painted to look like lions, puppies, tigers, and kittens. At the same moment, they both saw a short, round man struggling to ride a unicycle through the crowd. It was an impossible task. Every time he got on the bike and went a few feet, the crowd brought him to a halt and he fell off the bike. Shaking his fist at those in his way, he'd get on again and fall again, over and over. Zee and David leaned against each other, swaying with laughter. At moments like this, when they were perfectly in tune with each other, nothing else seemed to exist, and Zee could not imagine it ever being difficult between them. She wasn't sure how long it was after they lost sight of the man with the unicycle, but suddenly Zee felt a vibration in the crowd, a low, panicked hum that rose and crescendoed as it rippled toward them.

Zee sat up straight. It was exactly the scene that had been described by eye witnesses at the Paris seminar. "Shock bomb," she said. "I think it's a shock bomb."

They got into their Shock Socks as fast as they could and started the futile task of trying to halt the crowd. If any of them had been hit by the wave, running would only make their injuries worse. Even standing on the bench and yelling didn't work. The crowd was unstoppable. Telling Zee to stay where she was, David headed into the crowd to see if he could find the center of the blast. Zee had already called both police and ambulance and now, as the crowd began to thin, started attending to those who'd been left behind—children who'd gotten separated from their parents, a woman with a broken arm, others who'd fallen under the crowd's feet. Zee helped them one by one into their Shock Socks and gathered them together in a cluster by the bench. It was all unnecessary, she thought. No one had needed to run. No one did anything but make things worse by running. They all knew this. Yet despite the knowing, despite the public information campaigns and the drills and family discussions of what to do in case, they had all panicked and run. The anarchists' greatest ally, she thought, was human nature.

As the initial fear subsided, people began to flow back into the area. This was a different group from those who had fled, Zee realized. These people had been far enough away to be certain they hadn't been affected. They put their Shock Socks on anyway and headed for the bomb site, bent on helping in any way they could. Soon Zee had several volunteers following her directions.

David hadn't been able to determine the center of the blast zone but had been told the first bodies fell in the middle of Blackfriars Bridge—far enough away, with luck, not to have reached deep into the crowd around them. As he was explaining this, the first wave of ambulances began to arrive. Their way had been all but blocked by the crowds, and they were forced to travel in a long, slow caravan. Nevertheless, Zee felt a wave of relief when she saw them. She handed David a marker and told him to write a priority number on anyone he could, *1* for those who had been closest to the presumed center, *3* for those who'd been nowhere near, and *2* for everyone else.

She turned again to check the ambulances' progress and suddenly felt a wave of nausea and splitting headache pain. *Five, five, five* screamed in her head, and she found herself fixated on the fifth ambulance in the line. It looked exactly like all the other ambulances and yet she knew—*knew*—that everything about it was different. There was a bomb, but that was different too. It wasn't a shock bomb, something more old style.

A mental image of debris raining down flashed in her mind. She picked up the child closest to her and caught David's eye. "Run!" she screamed. She glanced at the child he was helping and hoped he understood. "Run!"

David managed to pick up two children and caught up with her. "Not toward the stalls—over there, behind that wall," he said, jerking his head toward a low stone wall.

They crouched down, sheltering the children with their bodies. It was an endless second before the ambulance, rigged with a conventional bomb and filled with nails and pieces of metal, exploded into the air. Zee remembered the same crushing nausea and splitting pain behind her eyes from the day she'd stood at Mr. Caldwell's bedside as shock bombs went off around the world. She recalled Rani's look of broad relief when Zee had told her it was a chance occurrence. And she remembered her adviser's words about the toll divining took on personal lives. This time, she wasn't going to tell anyone what she'd just felt. Not even David. People had lucky hunches all the time. This would just have to be one of them.

CHAPTER NINE

HAPPY BIRTHDAY

"Spill it, McAdams."

Zee was enjoying the artificial sunlight of the residence hall's courtyard. "No idea what you're talking about, Kapoor," she replied breezily, not bothering to close the book propped on her knees.

"Oh goodness," Rani said in a high-pitched cartoon voice. "Whatever might I mean?" Striking a pose of innocent confusion, her forefinger daintily tapping her chin, Rani was the spitting image of her third great-grandmother, a famous Bollywood star.

Laughing, Zee laid the book aside. Rani grabbed the little volume and held it up. "*Romeo and Juliet.*

What's this—our Zee reading for pleasure? Not *Further Thoughts on Diagnostic Empathy* or *Empathy and the Mind-Body Paradox*? This *is* serious."

Zee held out her hand. It was the volume David had given her that day at Brighton and she really didn't want to see it in anyone else's hand, not even Rani's. "I'll have it back, please. Some of us like to improve our minds, and I have two more acts to go."

"I'll save you the trouble—it doesn't end well." Rani leafed through the pages. "Let's see, end of third act, Mercutio—gone, Tybalt—gone. It doesn't get better, you know." She handed the book back and Zee tucked it safely away. "Why are you reading about star-crossed lovers anyway?"

Zee had been wondering that same thing herself. She wasn't sure if David had bought the book for its luxurious stamped leather binding, because it was one of the world's great plays, or to tell her something that was too painful to say in his own words. Or had he known that the hearts of the characters, whose world lay eight centuries in the past, would echo all the secrets her own heart held?

"It's just a story," she said at last.

Rani's eyes flashed with insight. "It's that boy, isn't it? The one who brought you and those kids in after the

Blackfriar's bombing and just *happened* to stay the whole night to work with you."

"He didn't stay to work with me. He was a volunteer. There were a lot of people who needed to be seen."

"Ri-ight," Rani said with exaggerated skepticism. "Well, he certainly seemed to need to see *you*. Now, I want all the details. And don't tell me you just met him, because that is so clearly not the case."

Zee wanted to tell Rani about David but hesitated. "He's an alien." For just a moment, Rani looked surprised. "Do you still want to hear?"

"Of course." Rani lifted her head and grinned. "I had no idea there were such cute aliens among us. What have I been missing? I'm going to have to rethink this whole thing. They can't possibly be that hot and be as nerdy as we thought. How did you meet him, and why didn't you tell me sooner?"

So Zee told Rani the whole story, including the part she was too embarrassed to tell Mrs. Hart, about the desire he ignited in her but didn't seem to share. "Maybe he just doesn't like me that way," she said.

"But he kisses you?"

"Mmm-hmm."

"And keeps seeing you?"

"Mmm-hmm."

"And it's more than a kiss on the cheek?"

"A lot more."

Rani tilted her head, considering the facts. "When he hugs you, where are his hands?"

"What?"

"Where does he put his hands? On your shoulders?"

"No, about here, I guess." Zee turned to indicate the small of her back.

"That clinches it, then. He's definitely into you."

"Really?"

"It's the hands. Arms and shoulders—no big deal. But hugging below the bra line—oh, yes, he's up nights thinking about you. Now all we need to do is get those hands of his a little more active."

"Rani!"

"I'm only thinking of your happiness. And have you told your parents yet?"

"Last night, and only because I had to. They wanted to come for my birthday and the holidays. They didn't want me to be alone. I had to tell them I wouldn't be, because he's taking me out."

"Where to?"

"He won't say, but he told me it's going to be a special night."

Rani gripped her arm. "Did he use those words? *Special night*? Those exact words?"

"Yeah, I think. I'm pretty sure."

"Then he's going to ask you back to his place! Oh my God, what are you going to wear? And what are we going to do with your hair? You'll need a *total* spa day—mani, pedi, the works. Maybe a haircut."

"Whoa," Zee said, recalling that it had been Rani who'd talked her into the pineapple haircut that had made the top of her head look like an erupting volcano. "Nothing drastic. I still want to look like me."

"You'll look exactly like you," Rani promised. "Only sexier."

By the time Zee left to meet David, she felt very nearly glamorous. She'd never felt glamorous before, but then, she'd never been seventeen before either. She couldn't afford a new dress, but Rani had raided her own bursting closet and found a midnight blue silk sheath that rippled like water and ended in a little flare just above the knees. Zee wasn't tall, but the way Rani had swept her hair up on top of her head made her feel tall.

It was mild weather for the end of the year, and there hadn't been this many people out in the West End since the bombings began. That morning the Prime Minister had announced that the suicide ambulance driver's apartment was yielding significant information about the anarchists' network, and that spark of good news had floated in the air like a champagne bubble all day long, touching everyone. As she walked toward the theater, Zee was aware of being looked at. Usually when she was out at night it was with Rani or some of the other empaths, and when boys looked at them and smiled or tried to start a conversation, their attention was directed to the group. But now Zee was alone, and it wasn't only boys who looked and smiled, it was young men David's age. Was this what being a woman was like? If it was, life was going to be great, Suddenly, an old-fashioned phrase of her dad's popped into her mind. *The world is your oyster.* She wasn't completely sure if it meant an oyster to eat or an oyster with a pearl inside, but whenever her father said it, he meant that life was going his way.

At first she couldn't find David in the crowd and wondered if she'd gotten the wrong theater, or was early or late. But then suddenly a sleek young man in a pale gray suit turned, and she saw that it was David. With his dark shirt and narrow white tie, slanting dark eyebrows above gray eyes, he could have been a hologram ad for bespoke suits or a movie holo for the latest heartthrob.

He kissed her hello. "You all set?"

"I can't wait," Zee said. She knew she sounded like a kid, but as they joined the crowd entering the theater, their reflection in the windows looked deliciously grown up.

David had waited until yesterday to tell her where they were going, and Zee knew he must have jumped through a lot of hoops and handed over a lot of cash to get tickets. The Thatcher Theater, nicknamed the Lady Meg, was London's newest theater, a seven-story counterpart to the New Empire in New York. The entire theater was the stage, and rows of seats broken apart, moved, and took flight to accommodate the action. Walls could turn into 3-D glaciers or vistas of a Beijing street market. When *Titanic!* played, the floor had parted to reveal the ocean and seats became watertight capsules that went down briefly with the ship, then popped to the surface and became lifeboats. But the show playing now, *Moonwalk*, was even more spectacular, and the hottest ticket in town. A musical about the first moon colony, it was performed in a weightless atmosphere as the audience watched from mobile pods. At the end, the audience was free to leave their pods and float down to ground level as the theater regravitized.

Zee giggled as David handed the usher—dressed in a cumbersome, tentlike suit reminiscent of the first moonwalkers—their tickets and said, "Space pod for two, please."

Inside, the pod was cozy and romantic, and David

put his arm around her as they floated to the top of the theater. The lights dimmed, and a voice came through the pod's soundfabric walls. Throughout the show, their pod would be flown by Mission Control. However, should they need to temporarily land for any reason, they only had to press the red emergency button. Now, if they were all ready: *ten, nine, eight, seven, ignition sequence started, six, five, four . . .*

And for the next two hours, Zee and David floated, cruised, ascended, descended, and hovered as actors zoomed around the theater's vast interior, singing and dancing. Well, not exactly dancing, Zee thought. You couldn't really dance in zero gravity. Instead, the actors formed complex human sculptures that changed effortlessly and continuously, like a kaleidoscope. At the end, as promised, the actors invited people to leave their pods and float down through the now-completed space station with them as gravity was slowly restored.

"You want to?" David asked.

"You bet."

They were seven stories up, floating near the ceiling, so it was hard to leave the pod, and some people turned back. But Zee didn't want to miss the experience, and finally took David's floating hand and swam into the air. They held hands all the way down and, magical as the experience was, it was good to feel the weight of David's arm around her shoulders again when gravity was completely restored.

"You choose the restaurant," David said afterward. "I love all your Earth food, so I'm not a good judge."

Zee hadn't been to the place she chose and didn't know if the food would be good or not, but it had candles on the tables and was the kind of restaurant she'd always dreamed of going to on a date. They agreed to order dishes they'd never heard of and had a good time trying to figure out what was in them. They shared dessert, even though both claimed they were too full to eat even a spoonful.

At last, pushing aside his plate, David laid a small gold box on the table.

"Happy birthday, Zee."

She wanted to say it was too much, that the theater tickets and dinner had cost dearly enough, but she saw his excitement and sudden shyness, and didn't want to do anything to spoil his pleasure in the evening he had planned. She slid the white ribbon off the box and lifted the lid.

"Oh. *Oh!* Are these—? Oh my gosh, they *are*— orbiting pearls!" Zee stared at the two perfect earrings, each one a tiny pearl stud with six more pearls circling the pearl nucleus. "Can I put them on now?" Carefully, she lifted one of the pearl studs and watched as the six circling pearls followed it like a flock of tiny, obedient doves. "How do I look?" she asked when they were both in place.

"You're beautiful, Zee. Just beautiful."

It was almost midnight when they left the restaurant, and Zee was glad she had the next two days off. The evening stretched like a long golden thread, drawing the two of them closer and closer together. David must have felt the same way, because as they walked, he held her close by his side and ruffled her hair with his lips, murmuring, "I can't let you go yet, Zee."

In his voice she recognized the deep, sweet longing she felt herself. She slid her arms around his waist and felt the warm tide of his pulse in the smooth muscles beneath the fabric. "Then don't let go of me yet, David. Don't let go of me ever."

They'd been walking for a while and were no longer entangled in the thick crowds of the West End. David stopped and turned her toward him. "Zee—"

"I mean it, David. I don't want to let you go either."

"We have to, Zee."

"Why?" She ignored the sadness in his eyes and kissed him again, a long unfolding that neither of them could stop. Again she felt the struggle within him, the wanting of her and the pushing away. "I want to be with you, David."

"Zee, please." He pulled away from her abruptly. "We can't be together."

Without his warmth, she felt the chill of the night air, and shivered. "Then why all of this?" she questioned, her voice rising. "The theater, the dinner, the earrings? Am I some kind of research project? Earth Girls 101? If you don't really like me—"

"I like you more than you can know, Zee. This has nothing to do with you."

The chill went away and anger suddenly flooded her chest, hot and burning. "*Nothing to do with me?* To you, maybe. To me, it has *everything* to do with me."

"I'm sorry," he said. He took a step toward her. "You're shivering. Let me put you in a cab and—"

"Don't bother!" Zee turned and walked as fast as she could, moving consciously into the shadows so he couldn't see her. She felt the first hot tear run down her cheek. This was the last thing she'd wanted to happen. She tried replaying the last few minutes in her mind, but it made no sense. How had everything gone so wrong so quickly?

Within a few blocks, she realized she had no idea where she was. She'd simply headed away from David into the dark, determined not to let him follow. Now she was alone on a dim, unfamiliar street. She couldn't have gone that far, she reasoned. She'd just walk until she came to a busy street, then find a cab and go home.

At first when the shadow rose up out of the darkness and rushed toward her, she thought it was David and felt a sweeping relief. But it wasn't. It was someone grabbing her purse and warning her not to make a sound. She couldn't see his face, but his shape was huge.

"Nothing more than this, love?" he asked, emptying the purse and tossing it aside, into the gutter. Not even your cash card? Or have you got that tucked away in that fancy dress of yours?"

Zee felt a tremor of icy fear but refused to give in to it. If he saw that she feared him, he'd know he could do anything to her. She couldn't outrun him, not in Rani's gray-strapped silver sandals, so she forced herself to raise her head and look him in the eye, or where she thought his eyes would be if she could see his face.

The motion must have caught the lamplight, because he said, "Ah, them pearly earrings all the girls are going for. They'll do me fine."

Her orbiting pearl earrings! *David's* earrings. His hand, huge and dirty, reached toward her. Until she heard her own piercing scream, she'd thought she was too terrified to make a sound.

"No!" she cried, reaching instinctively to protect the earrings.

She was never sure which she saw next, the flash of the knife blade or the second shadow, the one she knew was David, running toward them.

"No, David!" she cried. "He has a knife!"

"Shut up," the mugger yelled. As he whirled away from her, she felt a flash of pain skitter along her neck and collarbone.

The mugger held the knife in front of him, slashing the air in a way that made Zee dizzy.

He slashed savagely as he advanced and caught David at least once, Zee thought. But David, though unarmed, was younger and faster. In the end, he grabbed the mugger's wrist and twisted it until Zee heard a crunching pop. The knife clattered to the ground, and David kicked it away.

"If anything happens to her," he hissed, "I will find out who you are and I will destroy you. Do you understand?" He released the wrist, the hand now flopping at an odd angle, and the man fled into the darkness.

Zee felt cold, and when she touched her fingers to her throat and shoulder, her hand came away wet and sticky. She didn't remember sitting down on the curb, or how long David had been sitting beside her. She thought she must be delirious because David had his cell phone out and was talking urgently but calmly.

"I need you to take me offline. I'll explain when you get here. How long? Make it as soon as you can, I'm not sure how much time I've got. First aid kit—ours, not theirs—and make sure there's an accelerator in it. Clean clothes for me and one of your raincoats. I'll buy you a new one. Okay. Hurry."

"David?"

"Sssh, it's all right, Zee. Everything is going to be all right. Listen, do you trust me?"

She remembered the way he'd run toward the knife to save her and felt ashamed of the way she'd walked away from him. "I trust you," she said.

"Okay, that's good. Someone's coming to help us. I'm going to be sort of out of commission for a while. Do what she says, okay? If you trust me at all, do what she says."

As he talked, he was taking off his suit jacket. Zee saw the huge, spreading bloodstain on his shirt and gasped. Wincing, he stripped off the shirt, pressed it over the wound, and tied the sleeves around him to hold it in place. "Can you help me get the jacket back on? Let's go slow—you've lost some blood yourself. Okay. Two more things. Your residence hall—is there a guard or someone at the door? Can you pretend you're drunk long enough to get by him? Is there someone there you can trust?"

"Rani Kapoor," Zee said.

"Is there a way she could sneak me into the building and your room?"

She remembered Rani's joking complaints about Zee getting the room next to the outside window and smiled in spite of herself. "Are you kidding? This is just what she's been waiting for."

The next thing Zee remembered was David shaking her gently. "Cavalry's here."

Zee opened her eyes and found herself looking into a strangely familiar face. A face with delicate features framed by a waterfall of black hair.

"It's you," she said, too disoriented to be surprised.

David was trying to stand up but couldn't. "This is my research partner, Mia," he explained. "Also from Omura."

So she'd been right after all. The beautiful girl she'd seen hovering near so many times *was* connected to David. Only now that she saw them together, the romance she'd imagined didn't seem to be part of it.

David and Mia were talking, and Zee recognized the same quick, compressed speech David had used the night they met in A&E. Omuran, Zee now understood. If she had to guess, she would have said that Mia was asking David if he was ready, and when he said he was, she pulled him into an upright sitting position and bent his head forward. She pulled a small device from a zippered pocket of her jacket, held it just behind David's right ear, and fired two red beams into his head.

David's body went rigid for a second, then he slumped forward and would have toppled if Mia hadn't caught him and laid him down gently.

"You killed him," Zee gasped. "You *killed* him."

"Possibly," Mia said. "I don't think so, though. He should come around in a few minutes. Now, I'm going to find a taxi. When I come back, you and David are drunk, and I'm the responsible friend getting you both home, understand?" She started to walk away, then suddenly turned back and squatted down in front of Zee.

"One thing you should know," she said. "He just risked his life for you. He's been risking his life since he met you."

With that, she bounced up, zipped her leather jacket up to the chin, and disappeared into the darkness. Zee could hear her boot heels striking the sidewalk for a long time, and when they too vanished, she felt truly alone.

CHAPTER TEN

THE OUTLIER SPECIES

Zee was aware of swimming up through warm, heavy rivers of sleep. But each time she neared the surface, she dove back down. Once the darkness turned rosy against her eyelids and she knew it was daylight. She dove again, just for a few minutes, she told herself. When she swam up again, the rosiness was gone. It was evening, and this time she kept going until she broke the surface.

The last of the day's light came through the window high on her bedroom wall and from the small sitting room walls turned down low. She stood in the doorway.

"David?"

He was sitting on her couch. It seemed right that he was here, but she wasn't sure why.

For a moment, neither of them spoke. Then he crossed the room and put his arms around her. "I'm so sorry, Zee. I should never have let you walk away like that."

She noticed she was wearing scrub bottoms and an oversized T-shirt that said ROYAL LONDON LACROSSE, clothes she usually slept in. "Where are my real clothes? You—I—we didn't—?"

"No. Mia and Rani got you cleaned up and changed into those. *Before* Rani snuck me in. She's quite the watchdog where you're concerned."

Zee began to remember small bits and flashes but was having trouble piecing them together. "The beautiful girl. Mia? You asked me to trust her, and she helped us. She brought us here, right?"

"According to her, you made a fantastic drunk."

"Who is she?"

"My coworker. Another Omuran. I introduced you. Remember?"

"Who is she besides that? I've seen her before, like that day at Brighton, and you always know she's there but never introduce us. What's going on?"

He ignored her question. "And your friend Rani could be an actress. Mia said she came out into the lobby to get you and gave you the lecture of a lifetime, to make sure everyone would hear about it and leave you alone with your hangover for a few days. She brought some food, too. You should probably try to eat. You lost some blood, and I had to give you something to help you sleep."

Zee heard and felt again the sickening scrape of blade against bone. Cautiously, she touched her collarbone with her fingertips, then traced a line up her throat to her jaw. The skin was smooth and unbroken.

"I don't understand. The man with the knife . . . I'm sure he stabbed me. And you too. I can't have imagined it, there was blood all over your shirt."

David took her hand and slid it inside his shirt, her palm against his midriff. "He did stab me. Right about here. Feel it?"

"No." Zee felt nothing but smooth skin and muscle. No dressing, no wound. "How did you do this?"

He held up a small silver bar. Zee recognized it at once—it was just like the bar she thought she'd seen David put in his pocket the night they met in the emergency treatment room.

"An accelerator. It identifies damaged cells and kicks their repair rate into hyperdrive. These cells along your collarbone," he explained, "will always be a few weeks ahead of the rest in the aging process. You may get a wrinkle here first. Or, when you're a very, very old woman with dozens of descendants, there may be a slight discoloration or the hint of a sag."

His fingers moved from her collarbone to her throat and continued until they were buried in her hair. He drew her close, and she instinctively mirrored his movement, reaching up to twine her arms around his neck. She had to stand on her toes to do it, and felt the softness of her body unfold against his hard-muscled one. His dark hair, tousled over his forehead, was cut short at the back and trimmed close around his ears. She loved the way his skin went from rough to satiny, rough on his cheekbones and jaw, because he hadn't shaved, satiny on the back of his neck and earlobes.

For the first time, she realized he had a scar behind his right ear, a small, smooth circle no larger than a dime. As scars went, it was perfect, which was strange because scars were usually anything but perfect. Jagged, ridged, ugly, angry—that was the world of scars. This one seemed almost deliberate, a wound made with artistry in mind.

"David, what's this?" Her fingertip rested lightly on the spot.

"That's something I need to tell you about, Zee."

He paced back to the couch, drawing her with him.

His gray eyes, usually flecked with shards of amber, were clouded.

"What's wrong?" She touched his cheek, and the force of his thoughts nearly burned her palm.

"Everything. Everything I've done is wrong. I never meant to care so much for you, Zee. But that first night, in the emergency treatment room, I thought you were from Omura because we have so many redheads, and there're hardly any here. And even after I realized you weren't from Omura, you seemed like you were already part of me. There was something about your gestures, the way you moved and held yourself. It was like recognizing someone I cared for and hadn't seen for a long time.

"Seeing you even once was wrong—and dangerous—and I knew I couldn't let it happen again. I made a deal with myself that I could still see you without you knowing. Sort of keep track. Then there was the first shock bomb, and all I could think about was you and whether you were safe. I wasn't all that far from the blast. It was easy enough to find someone who needed to be checked out at a hospital. And easy enough to convince myself I was just being a good Samaritan. But it was about you, Zee. To make sure you were safe. It's always been about you."

She smiled softly. "I don't have a problem with that."

"But Omura does. Remember when I told you that our extreme efficiency has made most people opt out of having children and that our population is declining? It's a little more drastic than that. We no longer have enough people to sustain our civilization. Not enough workers to get everything done. Not enough young people to support the elderly who can no longer work. About a generation ago, there started to be food riots, and shortages of basic goods. The price of everything had shot up. There's a twenty-five-year waiting list for a house. A few decades years ago, forecasting models showed that our civilization was grinding to a complete halt and we would die out sometime within the next two hundred years. The Central Governing Authority passed the Emergency Repopulation Act. It's perfectly fair. Every citizen, no matter who, must marry and begin the reproductive process no later than his or her twenty-first birthday. I've had unusual freedom doing this work, but my twentieth birthday is coming up. That's when my name and bio go public on the government's Find-a-Mate service."

"What if you don't? Find a mate?"

"The government finds one for you. No one gets to be twenty-one without being married." David paused.

"Even if it weren't for that, Omura doesn't allow anyone to stay on assignment longer than two years. The risk of 'inappropriate attachments to the outlier species' is too great. Well, they were certainly right about that."

The thought of David with someone else, sharing his life and having children with someone else, piling up joys and sorrows and experiences with someone else until the memory of Zee was crushed and forgotten was an agony she'd never imagined. *This is impossible,* she thought. *No system could be so cruel.* Except for logical, for-the-good-of-the-whole Omura.

"Are you—do you have someone already? Is it Mia?" Zee could not help driving the lit match into the open wound. Who wouldn't love Mia? Tall, beautiful Mia. Lucky Mia, who would spend her whole life with David.

"Mia? Cripes, no. She's like a sister or something. She's been the reason you and I have been able to see each other at all."

"I don't understand."

"That scar you felt? Behind my ear? I'm chipped, Zee. We all are. The chip continuously feeds my coordinates back to Omura. If I were to have gone all the places we went together on my own, it would have aroused suspicion. But as long as Mia showed up in the vicinity, her chip would relay back the same coordinates, and they'd assume we were together."

"That was nice of her."

David laughed lightly. "Payback. Believe me, I've done the same thing for her plenty of times."

Another detail from the night before drifted back to Zee—an image of Mia shooting two red beams of light into David's head, just where the chip was.

"And that thing she used on you? You went rigid. I thought you were dead."

"Mia's own invention," David said. "She calls it the Stunner."

"What does it do?"

"Chips aren't the most stable form of technology. They're vulnerable to bad data, scrambled firmware, even local viruses. They go offline all the time for no reason. Mia's Stunner takes a chip offline deliberately, without anyone on Omura knowing why. Once you're offline, they can't track you until they reconfigure the chip and rebuild the data, which takes about thirty-six hours. Then they own you again."

"David?

"Mmm?" His voice was almost sleepy, as if his story had exhausted him.

"If it isn't Mia, is there someone on Omura? Someone you want to go back to?"

"No."

"Then stay here. Earth is a good place. When it's time to go back, stay here."

"It isn't allowed, Zee. No one escapes the Repopulation Act."

"Have Mia take you offline. We'll run away."

"They'd rebuild the chip."

"Can't you have the chip removed?"

"Only if my brain comes with it. It, uh, grows little filaments, like tentacles, throughout the cortex."

"That's barbaric."

"It's efficient. And that's what Omura is all about. Efficiency."

"What if you just refused to go back? We could explain what's going on. It's a violation of your rights. We'd give you sanctuary here."

He sighed a slow, heavy sigh. "It wouldn't do any good, Zee. In fact, it would make things worse. If they ever find out about us, they'll kidnap me and erase you, as an example to everyone else. I've put you in enough danger already. I never meant to, but I've never felt like this about anyone before."

"Me either."

"Then I'm doubly sorry. And I'm going to try to repair the damage." He stood up and started gathering things scattered on the table. The accelerator, a video cube, the alien ID he was required never to be without. He carried a cereal bowl and plate to the sink, washed them, and set them carefully on the counter.

"What are you doing, David?"

"What I should have done months ago. Getting out of your life before they find out about you."

"It's not fair!" she cried.

"I know it isn't. The Central Governing Authority—"

"I don't mean the Central Governing Authority, I mean you! *You're* not fair."

"Zee—"

"You can't make all the decisions for us. Not if you really care about me." She waited until her breathing slowed to normal. "Please. You won't be back online until tomorrow afternoon. Stay. Hold me. Just for tonight." She took his hand and met his gaze. "My decision. No matter what happens. *My* decision. Understood?"

He nodded slightly. "Do you always get your own way like this?" he asked, unable to hide a faint, dawning smile.

"I don't really know," she said triumphantly. "I've never wanted my own way all that much. Just with you."

"Me too," he said, beginning a kiss that started at her temples and swept all the way down to her throat. "Just with you."

No one had ever kissed her throat before. Who

knew it would make her so delirious with pleasure that when he pulled away from her she almost fell over?

"I nearly forgot about these," he said, pulling from his pocket the small gold box he'd given her the night before.

"Oh! My orbiting pearl earrings! I thought the mugger took them and I'd never see them again." She opened the box and saw the little pearls orbiting each of the central pearls. "And look! Not a pearl lost!"

He put his arms around her, then tapped the wall until the light faded to the faintest blue glow. "That's the thing about orbiting pearls," he murmured. "They always find each other. No matter what pulls them apart."

Four hours later, David stood at the end of the bed, fully dressed and looking down at Zee. He was memorizing all the things he loved about her. The way her dark red hair flowed across the pillow like a river running over its banks. The fact that her eyes weren't blue or green, like most redheads, but the color of cherry cola and that the arch of her eyebrows made it seem that life itself was a continual surprise to her.

Beside her on the nightstand, next to her orbiting pearl earrings, lay the eagle medallion she'd given him.

He'd known at once that it must have cost her dearly—empaths didn't earn all that much, and she'd talked about a pair of sandals with moonstones that she'd wanted but ended up without. That she'd bought the medallion then been too shy to give it to him right away made him treasure it all the more. He hoped she'd know this when she saw that it was gone. As quietly as he could, he removed it from the nightstand and slipped the leather thong over his head.

Zee thought because he was older he knew about all the things she didn't—he saw it in her eyes. But really, they were so much alike. He'd never been in love before either. Now, looking down at her, he wondered how he could ever love someone this much again. And he wondered what she would say if she knew the truth—the *real* truth—about him, and why he was visiting her world.

CHAPTER ELEVEN

WITHOUT WARNING

Zee knew David was gone the minute she woke up. She no longer felt his warmth at her back or the weight of his arm across her hip. When she slid one foot backwards, it found only cool, empty sheets. Opening her eyes, she saw her orbiting pearl earrings on the nightstand, but the eagle talisman beside them was gone. Seeing the empty space was like hearing a door closing.

She searched the sitting room hoping to find even the smallest sign that he meant to return. She'd hoped that spending the night together would change things. It had for her. Nested in the circle of his arms, waking and turning to find him still there, she'd never felt so close to anyone in her life, or so safe. It made her believe that together they could overcome any obstacle.

And it broke her heart to know he would never feel the same. The night hadn't changed anything for him. He left because he'd decided it was too dangerous for them to be together. If he'd meant to come back, he wouldn't have taken the eagle talisman.

Slowly, Zee sat down on the sofa and drew herself into a tight ball. She already ached to feel his arms around her again. How, she wondered, was she going to live the rest of her life without that?

A few days before her birthday, lines of an old song had come to her and been playing over and over in her head ever since. *I'm not a girl who loves forever—just until the sun leaves the sky, just until the sea runs dry. . . .* She hadn't heard it since she'd come to London and had no idea why she was thinking of it now, except the *just until*s were how she felt about David. Whether he was here or not, she would love him forever. Knowing it was foolish and superstitious, she made the song her ringtone.

For the next six weeks, Zee felt as if she were sleepwalking. Work was the only place she felt alive, and she volunteered for so many extra shifts her adviser became concerned. Rani was concerned too, but fell silent when Zee said she wasn't ready to talk about it. Instead, Rani deflected questions about her friend by saying Zee was still embarrassed about binge drinking the night of her birthday.

Then one evening Zee came home to find a note under her door, hand printed in block letters with no signature.

I KNOW WHAT YOU'RE GOING THROUGH, AND I CAN HELP. MEET ME TOMORROW AT THE SUNRISE CAFÉ. 7AM.

The rush of elation was instant. The note could only be from David, or from Mia delivering David's message. It certainly wasn't from Rani, and they were the only ones who knew what had happened the night of her birthday. To eliminate any doubt, he'd chosen the café he took her to that first morning.

When she thought about it, she wasn't even surprised. Part of her had known all along that he wouldn't be able to give her up, any more than she could give him up. They were meant to be together. Nothing would ever change that. For the first time since he'd left, she felt like she had her life back.

The next morning, she arrived at the café early. She

wanted to make sure she got the same booth they'd had before and ignored several empty ones until it was free. Settling herself with ten minutes to spare, she let herself look forward to the day ahead. Her shift didn't start until three that afternoon, an eternity away. She and David could stroll all over the city, hand in hand. They could buy a picnic lunch and find someplace romantic to eat it. They could go to a museum or a movie or—

"Zee! I almost didn't see you here!"

Zee looked up to find Piper staring down at her. The last person she wanted to bump into. She looked around quickly and was relieved to see that David hadn't arrived yet.

"Piper. I'm actually, um, wai—" Before she could finish speaking, Piper sat down across from her.

"Why did you pick a booth so far back? I couldn't even see you at first."

It was at that moment Zee realized where the note had come from.

"Piper? *You* left the note under my door?"

"I know all the signs of lovesickness," she said, "a certain kind of lovesickness in particular. Believe me, I'm an expert. So I thought if we could talk—"

Zee heard nothing past "lovesickness." A red veil of disappointment and anger descended. Piper had taken the most private thing in her life and dragged it out in the open. Piper, who claimed to be sorry for setting her up with David in the first place, as a kind of joke, now proved she wasn't sorry at all.

"I can't believe you're doing this," Zee said, leaping to her feet and gathering her things. "Are you that bitter about your own life? Do you *enjoy* doing this? What have I ever done to you, anyway?"

"No, wait, you've got it wrong, Zee. I only want to help. You don't understand, please—"

Zee was on her way out the door. She didn't feel like understanding, but stopped to look back over her shoulder at Piper.

"The only way you can help is by leaving me alone!" she cried, and rushed out of the café and back to the safety of her room at the residence hall. Only then, lying on her bed, did she contemplate the real source of her despair—that the note hadn't been from David at all, and she'd been mistaken in thinking he couldn't give her up.

Once again, Zee threw herself into her work. She especially looked forward to seeing Mrs. Hart, even though each time she visited the Hampstead house, she confronted changes. Mrs. Hart was definitely losing weight and often leaned on Zee to take more than a few steps.

Yet despite the weight loss and the weakness, Mrs. Hart seemed more herself than ever and still greeted Zee in her Neptune's Tears. "They came at such a great price, you see," she commented one day. "It seems an insult to hide them away."

Their sessions divided into two parts, which Mrs. Hart referred to as "homework" and "bunking off." During the homework part, Zee helped Mrs. Hart with images that allowed her body to relax and tap into its reserves. What they both liked best, though, was bunking off. Zee loved sitting in Mrs. Hart's kitchen and talking about whatever came to mind. The kitchen, like the rest of the house, seemed like an extension of Mrs. Hart herself. Today Mrs. Hart served chocolate biscuits on plates shaped like autumn leaves and poured tea from a pot shaped like a gourd.

"I wanted to use these one last time," she said. "I made them while I was pregnant with my first daughter, and they've always been my favorites."

After Neptune's Tears, Ellie Hart's name became as famous—and as unlucky—as the diamonds her name would be forever linked to. No one would hire her as a designer, yet her house was full of beautiful things she had created for the pure joy of making them. Studying the delicate glaze on her maple leaf dish, Zee said, "I'm sorry you never got your design career."

Mrs. Hart's eyes flashed. "Are you?" she asked tartly. "Don't be. I'm not."

Zee had never seen Mrs. Hart show irritation before, and realized she'd said the wrong thing. "I didn't mean—"

"Never mind, dear. I'm just having a bad moment because of the pain today." Mrs. Hart was thoughtful for a moment. "I was a newlywed in America when I won the Neptune competition. My husband got a job promotion to come here to London. If everything had worked out, I was going to stay in the US without him. When you're young, you take love for granted. You think, if it's meant to be, it will take care of itself. That isn't so at all. Looking back, I'm sure that if things had gone according to plan with the diamonds, my marriage would have paid the price. It's true that I never had the career I thought I'd won, but I had a long, happy marriage, and I had my daughters. That's been one of the nicer surprises about life, that no matter what you lose, there are always good things to be had."

She knew Mrs. Hart was telling her this for a reason. Just a few minutes ago, Zee had given her a slightly sugarcoated version of what had happened with David, tears and all.

"I know what you're thinking," Mrs. Hart continued. "You're thinking it's easy for me to say because everything is settled. Well, you're right in that. It's been a century since I was your age, but I do remember what it's like, all that uncertainty and doubt. And you're thinking of that young man of yours, aren't you? The one who ran off without a trace?"

Zee nodded "I can't imagine never seeing him again." *Even if it costs my life*, she added silently.

Ellie Hart laid her hand over Zee's. "There are times, dear, when nothing short of following one's heart will do. Give your heart time, Zee. It will tell you what to do."

Time? Zee couldn't imagine spending more days in the turmoil she'd been in since David left. "What do I do until then?"

"Ah," said Mrs. Hart. "That one's easy. When you can't be of use to yourself, be useful to others. Keep the forward momentum going."

Two nights later was Zee's regular Friday overnight shift. Halfway through her three A.M. break, her hand-held began to vibrate. *Want 2 assist Ob case?* It was from Dr. Onyongo, whom she'd done a maternity rotation with. Though empaths all did a stint in obstetrics, they seldom got called in on cases until they had more experience and advanced training. Births were tricky because two lives were involved, and it wasn't always easy to separate the tangled impulses of mother and child. Zee lost no time.

B there in 5, she typed back.

"I was relieved to see your name on the duty list tonight, Zee," Dr. Onyongo said. "We only have one OB empath on, and she's handling a complicated multiple birth. Here's the bullet. Patient is two or three hours away from delivery and proceeding fine, except she's literally terrified of giving birth. She's so afraid of ripping and tearing that she's guaranteeing herself just that unless she can relax. You remember how the tissues have to stretch and relax to let the baby's head emerge?"

Zee nodded.

"Good. That's what we need to let happen here. I sent her patient notes to your handheld. See what you can do, and I'll stop by in twenty minutes or so to check progress."

Zee loved the way Dr. Onyongo could convey information so rapidly without seeming rushed or impatient. It was her voice, Zee decided, low and musical and calm. It made her want to visit Kenya, where Dr. Onyongo was from, to see if everyone talked like that.

She did a double take when she saw the patient's name, Clara Miller. Of course, there must be dozens of Clara Millers in the UK, probably at least a dozen in

London alone. But the case notes made it clear—this was *the* Clara Miller, the first woman swimmer to win five gold medals in a single Olympics. Zee had been eleven at the time and idolized her. Now she was going to help deliver her baby.

Dr. Onyongo hadn't exaggerated. Clara Miller's short, dark hair framed her white, clenched face against the pillow, and her knuckles, gripping the bed rail, were blotched with white. The only spot of color in the room was a vase of fuchsia gladioli.

"Beautiful flowers," Zee said, trying to gauge the vibe in the room. Obstetric empaths seldom met their patients in advance. They had to build a connection quickly and get to work as fast as possible.

"They're from my husband," Clara said. "He's on his way, but he was coaching at the South African world finals and won't be here in time. I can't—I don't think I can do this without him."

Zee didn't argue. She already had a different strategy in mind. "The world *swim* finals? Oh my God, is your husband Jeff McDonald? And you're Clara Miller?" She sounded surprised, even to herself. Some patients felt spied on if they knew you'd read their records, and letting a natural conversation unfold built trust. "I can't believe it! I had a Clara Miller gym bag and a Clara Miller suit and goggles, even a towel, I think. I had everything Clara Miller except your backstroke. I never could do it. My dad was so patient—he'd float me on the water, and I'd be cartwheeling along—then I'd realize his hands weren't under me anymore and go down like a stone."

Clara's face brightened as if to say, *Oh, this*—this *is something I understand!* "Common scenario," Clara said. "And it's not too late, you know."

"I think it might be," Zee said. "I tend to panic on my back."

"Let me guess—your hips go down first, right? And you kind of fold up?"

"You've got it," Zee said, though nothing like that had ever happened to her. She'd taken to the backstroke like a duck to water. "That's just what happens. What am I doing wrong?"

"You're fighting the water," Clara said. "When you were a kid and thought your dad was supporting you, it was really the water. You relaxed into it and let it carry you. But when you realized your dad wasn't there, you fought the water, and the instinctive move on that one is to fold up like a clam." A bit of color had come back into Clara's face. "You can never win fighting the water. You have to go with it."

"I'll try to remember that next time," Zee said.

Clara gave a little laugh. "Call me if you need a

reminder. Oh—oh—here comes another labor pain." She gritted her teeth and gripped the bed rail so hard Zee could see the tendons in her arm tighten.

"Tell you what," Zee said. "Think of it as a wave. Big, blue wave. Relax into it and let it carry you."

When Clara's breathing slowed and evened, Zee knew that the contraction had passed. "Was that easier?"

"Actually, it was. Still hurt like holy hell, though. Don't tell anyone I said that. The press loves to catch celebrities swearing. Very embarrassing."

"Your secret's safe," Zee assured her.

Dr. Onyongo arrived in time for the next contraction. "You're progressing well," she told Clara. "How're you doing with the contractions? Still begging for a C-section?"

"No, I think I can do this now."

"Great work, Zee." Dr. Onyongo glanced at the clock on the wall. "I think you can go back now, but if you swing by the nursery in three or four hours, the baby should be here."

"You're sending her *away*? Please, can't she stay? Since my husband isn't going to be here, I really need someone. Please?"

Zee had helped during hard labor before, but she'd never been at an actual birth. Three hours and sixteen minutes later, when the blue blanketed bundle of baby boy was put into Clara's arms, Zee felt as tired and exhilarated as anyone else in the room. No wonder they called it labor, she thought.

"Isn't he beautiful?" Clara beamed.

Despite the baby's slightly pointy head and face like a squinched-up rose, Zee was surprised at just how beautiful he was.

Later, walking away down the corridor, Zee realized that her face was wet with tears. Dr. Onyongo said it was a common response, something that had to do with female hormones. That didn't seem like a big enough explanation to Zee. Right now, Clara Miller's baby was losing himself to baby concerns. *I'm tired. Where did that breast go? I like the way she holds me.* But Zee had been there when he'd arrived from parts unknown, wrapped in layers of mystery. Hours ago, in a place without hours, he'd floated in a firmament of stars. What kind of world had been his then? What dreams had he brought, so magnificent the merest flashes would carry him through an entire existence?

Her tears were tears of awe.

Tomorrow morning, Clara's husband would arrive and see his son for the first time. At this thought, Zee felt the divesting wall, the mental barrier that separated her self from her work, begin to crumble. It was impossible to imagine that reunion and not envy Clara. Her life was so settled, the path to happiness so clear, whereas Zee's own life was anything but clear. She wondered if she would ever have what Clara had. Not on this planet, she thought with a sudden sense of longing. Not with David. Her longing became a knife point and her tears began in earnest.

By the time Zee got home, it was seven thirty A.M., and all she wanted was the comfort of sleep and maybe a hologram running in the background. She activated the wall screen and scrolled through several pages before she settled for catching up on back episodes of *Survivor: The Mars Edition*. She drifted off to people yelling about freezing temperatures and no drinking water and woke up to the same thing. Except that the yelling she woke up to sounded much more desperate, and it soon became apparent that she'd left the realm of reality holovision and was getting the live news default channel.

"Every building!" a woman was saying in accented English. "The Corniche, the roads, every building within at least a mile inland. All of Beirut is gone. The dust and debris are so thick you can see nothing, not even the sun."

Zee sat bolt upright. It was the song, the one that had been playing in her head since before her birthday, *Until the sun leaves the sky.*

"For those of you just joining us, we're continuing with live coverage of the Beirut earthquake. Striking at eight fourteen this morning, the quake, now estimated at nine-point-five on the Richter scale, leveled virtually all of Beirut's buildings and caused a massive tsunami throughout the Mediterranean area. Here again is the stunning footage taken by a news crew from their studio on Mount Lebanon."

Zee found herself staring at a panoramic view of a beach—only the beach extended for what looked like miles, taking up the space where the sea should have been. *Until the sea runs dry.*

Along the beachfront, thousands of people gathered, hypnotized by the sight. More and more people joined them, though whether it was to escape the ruined buildings or to look at the eerily empty sea wasn't clear. A thin dark line appeared on the far horizon and rapidly thickened, sweeping toward the beach with alarming speed. The crowd now turned and tried to run to higher ground, but was blocked by the human tide still arriving. The black line of the tsunami rushed forward, and Zee, unable to look away, watched as it engulfed thousands of people and slammed inland with them.

"The main wave was an estimated 180 feet, traveling at speeds in excess of 600 miles per hour," the presenter was saying. "As might be expected, the majority of those on the beach are now feared dead. To recap, the quake struck without warning at eight fourteen this morning and lasted for approximately one minute, leveling most of Beirut and its suburbs. Red Cross and Red Crescent agencies worldwide are banding together to send aid. Thought to be stronger and certainly more lethal than Beirut's legendary AD 551 earthquake . . ."

Zee could not get the phrase *struck without warning* out of her head. There *had* been a warning. She had received it in the song that kept running through her head, but she'd been so caught up in her own concerns she'd been blind. Before she could change her mind, she looked up the number for the Psi Center and made an appointment to be tested.

CHAPTER TWELVE

JOURNEYS

Almost half a million people had been killed in the earthquake and tsunami. Zee wrote the number on a card and put it in her wallet as a reminder. She never again wanted to feel as useless as she'd felt watching the tsunami wash over Beirut. Empathy was a skill that many people had an affinity for and a fair number chose to develop. There was no shortage of empaths in the world. There was, however, a shortage of diviners. No matter what her adviser had said about the choice being hers, the misinterpreted song and its devastating consequences had changed everything. If she had abilities that could be developed to save even one life, there was no choice.

She knew very little about the tests themselves. She'd been told only that they'd take the better part of a day and she shouldn't plan on doing anything strenuous that evening. Zee, who did fine *with* patients but not so well *as* a patient, began to imagine mild electronic shocks and needles extracting blood. To calm herself as she walked toward the building, she thought of the evening ahead. She and Rani had agreed to have a night in, just like they used to when they were students. Only now they had salaries, so instead of fish and chips—or sometimes just chips—Zee planned to pick up two orders of artichoke alfredo, garlic bread, and stuffed mushrooms on the way home. Rani was in charge of entertainment and pudding, and had told Zee she'd laid in a basket of fresh strawberries, three different kinds of cream, series one of *Stranded!* and this year's Best of Janies winner, *Punk and Prejudice*. And at some point in all this, Zee was going to enlist Rani's help in what she'd come to think of as plan A, the next step in her personal life. Rani already knew Zee was testing this afternoon, and the awed, slightly gobsmacked look had returned to her face. That plus a lot of whipped cream and strawberries would probably win her cooperation.

The offices of the Psi Center were bland to the point of arousing Zee's suspicion. Everything in the reception area existed in a narrow color spectrum, ranging from cream to pale caramel. But the person who greeted Zee and introduced himself as Colonel Hamish Dawson, Special Air Service Counterterrorism and Anarchy, retired, offered a completely logical explanation.

"We don't want to inadvertently seed people's minds and skew the results," he said, leading her down a long corridor. "We work with a lot of international anti-terrorist forces, you know, and have a lot of military on staff. Some government efficiency expert came around once and hung a lot of battle scenes and whatnot on the walls, to 'make us feel as one.' A greater mental maelstrom you have never seen. We didn't get reliable readings for over a month. Well, here we are, then."

He led her into a small office and motioned her to a chair. Zee was relieved to note that they hadn't passed any medical-looking rooms. "I'll be supervising your tests today, but let's get to know each other a bit first."

What followed was a conversation Zee recognized as a verbalized version of a codified personality test designed to weed out subjects whose temperament or whose motives were unsuitable. Did she realize the work was essentially unpaid? That any work she did would become property of the Psi Center and/or its clients? That the government would necessarily open and maintain a file on her? That should her identity become known, she would most likely get death threats? And finally, why did she want to become a diviner?

"Actually, I don't," Zee answered. She told him how happy she was being an empath, and how three incidents had intruded on this happiness—the day in the hospital when she caught the thoughts and emotions of victims of the simultaneous shock bombings, the day at Blackfriars Bridge when she'd known beyond a doubt that the fifth ambulance in line had a bomb in it, and most recently, the tsunami. "I'd rather this wasn't happening, but since it is, if there's a way it can help people, well . . . at least there's a purpose."

There were a dozen different tests, all of which she did more than once in what Colonel Dawson called "runs." Some of the tests were fascinating and absorbing, more like puzzles or games, while some were so pointless they made her want to scream. Like predicting what a card dealt from a deck would be or picking five winning lottery numbers from a grid. These two in particular irritated her, and of course they were the ones Colonel Dawson wanted to do ten runs of each. Other tests were more interesting, like one where an office envelope containing a picture was placed in front of her and she was asked to describe it in words or by sketching it without opening the envelope or peeking at the picture.

Her two favorite tests involved large transparent boxes. The first one Colonel Dawson referred to as the Cube. Lying on the bottom of an empty Plexiglas box measuring about a foot on each side was a glowing, cherry red disk. When Zee slipped on a pair of membrane-thin sensor gloves, she could move the disk by moving her hands. Colonel Dawson asked her to think of the box as a large area, like an office building.

"A target has already been placed there at random but is hidden from you at present," he explained. "Imagine the target is a hostage who needs to be rescued and place the disk next to where you believe the hostage is."

Zee did, and when the red disk was where she wanted it, pressed a button. A blue disk instantly appeared just a few centimeters away. Zee's results were so unusual that after a run of ten the colonel asked her to repeat the test. Of her first ten trials, the cherry disk was almost exactly on top of the blue one in half of them. In the other half, it was almost as far away as it could be.

"I think you're trying to predict where the target will be," the colonel explained. "So if it was in the top right one time, you think it will be in the lower left the next. But the target is placed totally at random. It could as easily be in exactly the same place the next time. Try not to predict where it might be. Just feel where it is."

Zee tried to follow his advice, which wasn't easy. How could you feel something in an empty space? You had to clear your mind and act on pressures so slight it was impossible to be consciously aware of them. On the second round, she wasn't sure if she was finding a way into the problem or simply guessing and placing the disk rapidly out of frustration. Whether it was skill or luck, she improved the success rate to seven out of ten.

But it was the final test that was her favorite. Colonel Dawson brought out another Plexiglas box shaped like an oversized shoebox and nearly a meter in length. It was completely empty. Unlike the Cube, there was no glowing disk inside and no pair of gloves to wear. The test must have been the colonel's favorite because he set it in front of her with a flourish, as if he were a waiter serving a slice of thirteen-layer chocolate cake.

"And now," he announced, "my little theater. In the scenes you're about to see, danger is lurking. One of the characters is up to no good and means the others harm. Watch carefully and try to spot the culprit before he—or she—acts. When you do, press this button."

Zee wasn't sure what she expected, but what

she saw when Colonel Dawson activated the box made her gasp. Instantly, an entire section of Oxford Street appeared in miniature in 3-D, with traffic and buses and people going about their business. It was so real-looking—much more substantial than most holograms—that it was difficult to believe the miniature people weren't real. Reminding herself of her assignment, she began scanning the crowd. Within a few seconds, a shock bomb went off and people began to run. Horrifyingly, a few dozen piled up at the end of the box and suffocated.

"Don't worry," Colonel Dawson said. He tapped his handheld, and the box cleared, bodies, red buses, and all. "The only person who ever got the first one was a psychopath, unsuitable for all sorts of reasons. Let's try again."

This time Zee focused on the action, freezing the drama when she thought she'd identified the culprit. But she'd picked wrong, and when Colonel Dawson resumed the action, the mother with a baby carriage turned out to be a suicide bomber.

"You're trying to use logic and deduction," he told Zee. "Forget that. Just go with your vibe."

She tried and got one of the next three right, which the colonel told her was quite good. But when he asked her what had led to her "vibe," as he called it, she couldn't say. Then they broke for lunch—Branston pickle with cheese, a combination Zee was certain she'd never get used to—then reviewed the results of the tests.

"Well, Miss McAdams," Colonel Dawson began, "you've demonstrated a singular inability to predict the future in a wide range of circumstances."

"Oh." Zee felt surprisingly let down. In spite of her reluctance about becoming a diviner, she'd wanted to do well. She began to gather her things.

"*But*," he continued, "on the most crucial tests you exhibited unusually high potential. Would you like to hear more?" Zee relaxed back into her chair and the colonel smiled. "The tests you did the worst on were the gambling tests—the lottery and card prediction. The rapidity with which you completed these compared with other tests indicates an element of moral judgment."

"Isn't that a good thing?"

"Perhaps in some cases," the colonel said thoughtfully, "but here we work as one organism, without room for individual judgment. In most cases, you won't be told what you're looking for. A target could be anything from a hostage to a loose nuke. This ensures that your perceptions will be as pure and spontaneous as possible, uncontaminated by expectations. So our requests will not always make sense, and may even seem dubious, but we count on you to take them seriously."

"Fair enough," said Zee.

The last test they reviewed was the one Colonel Dawson called *viewing*, where Zee had been asked to describe a picture that was concealed from her.

"Wrong every time," the colonel announced cheerfully. "But there's a method to our madness. Let's try this one again. There's a picture in this envelope. We asked you what you saw. Do you remember what you said?"

"A ladder."

"Ah. Now, clear your mind. No more ladder. Tell me, what kind of lines do you see?"

"Straight," Zee said without hesitation. "Long. Vertical. But not quite parallel. Closer together at the top than the bottom."

"Colors?"

"Mmm. Gray. Like metal or stone. But there's white between the gray lines. Something . . . a cloud?"

"Don't think specific objects, just their properties."

Zee nodded and tried again. "Something light. Not just a light color. *Light*—airy."

The colonel slid the envelope across to her. "Have a look."

Zee pulled out the picture. "Wow." Every element she'd named was there. Only her conclusion that it was a ladder was wrong. The two long gray lines, closer together at the top than the bottom turned out to be the rocky sides of a waterfall. The lightness she'd misread as space between the steps was a misty fall of white water.

"You just went from an F on this to an A-list candidate. Interested?"

Zee hadn't felt such a rush of excitement since her early training as an empath. "When can I start training?"

"You just did. We train by putting you on actual assignments, working with a large team. Since it's more or less volunteer, the schedule is flexible. I do have one warning, though."

"What?"

"If you're in this for the perks, the tuna salad and Branston pickle are as good as it gets. Other than that, you have the chance to do a great deal of good here. See those file cabinets? The first is letters from parents of missing children we've managed to locate. The next is anarchist attacks averted. The rest is miscellaneous—hostages freed, stolen art masterpieces located, missing top-secret documents, stolen weapons." He reached across his desk and clasped her hand. "Welcome."

By the time Zee got to Rani's room at the residence hall, laden with takeaway bags of artichoke pasta and garlic bread, Zee was mentally exhausted. There was nothing she wanted more than to sit on Rani's sofa and watch her friend set out bowls, silverware, soft drinks, and grated cheese, all while carrying on a running commentary about a patient she'd had that day who not only wanted Rani to work with her but with her pet ferret in "group sessions." The patient had diabetes and insisted that the ferret, though perfectly healthy, had a tendency to be "an enabler where sweets were concerned."

"How is that possible?" Zee asked, laughing. "It's not like the ferret is popping out to the shops for Maltesers."

"That's where you'd be wrong," Rani said, bringing the bowls to the sofa and handing Zee one. "According to my patient, the ferret has a subscription to the Chocolate of the Month Club."

They tucked their feet up and slurped up the pasta. They used to have evenings like this all the time when they were students, and had taken them for granted. Now Zee looked back on those times as special and saw that they would become more and more rare as each of them was claimed by other people and other demands.

As if reading her thoughts, Rani set her empty bowl aside and said, "So. I agreed to meet that boy my auntie Meera has been talking about. The one who is coming to England this fall to start at the London School of Economics."

"What's this? Are you becoming the good Hindu girl you swore you'd never be?" Zee couldn't imagine anything less Rani-like than an arranged meeting.

Rani shrugged. "I suppose it's inevitable." She dipped her head but could not hide her half smile. "Besides, he sent me his picture and a long letter. Both were very charming."

"Especially the picture?" Zee guessed.

"Something like that." Rani giggled. "He has navy blue eyes. It's true! I think he must have an English grandparent or something."

Zee drew a deep breath. Now was as good a time as any. "Speaking of boys, I have a favor to ask you. But it's, umm, a little bit dodgy, so promise you'll say no if you don't want to do it."

Rani raised her eyebrows. "Zee McAdams breaking the rules? I like it already."

"I need to see David. Even if he's right that it's too dangerous for us to keep seeing each other. I need to know he really means it. And I don't even know where he lives in London. He never gave me his address."

"And that's where I come in?"

Zee nodded. "Do you hate the whole idea?"

"Why would I?"

"Because he's an alien, because just the other day you said, 'I can't imagine getting that upset over a boy.' "

Rani looked wounded. "That's right, Zee. I said *I—I* can't imagine. But that doesn't mean it's wrong for you. Maybe I think it's kind of cool that you can throw yourself into it like that. Maybe I'd like to feel that way about someone sometime."

Zee had spoken too harshly and was sorry. Before she could say anything, Rani went on graciously, "Now, tell me what the plan is."

"Are you still working A&E shifts? That first night he was brought in, I'm sure they must have looked at his papers and done a standard admittance. But that patient privacy firewall is impenetrable. You can't get into it without a doctor's PIN."

Rani grinned. "No problem. There's a new intern there who claims he'd do anything for a date with me. Let's let him prove it."

"You don't mind? Dating this guy just to get me that address?"

"Oh, I was going to go out with him anyway," Rani said. "This will just make it all the more special for him."

"Wouldn't it be more special if he knew you were going out with him because you like him?"

Rani gave an exasperated sigh. "You really *don't* know anything about men, do you, Zee?"

Rani had the address within forty-eight hours, and Zee spent every free minute of the next few days watching an unobtrusive building on a moderately busy north London street. Fortunately, there was a bus stop across the way, so she could hide herself in the waiting queue. It wasn't until early evening of the third day that she saw Mia sweeping down the street, her rapid walk and waterfall of glossy hair unmistakable. Zee hurried to catch her before she disappeared inside the building.

"Mia? Please, I need to talk to you."

Mia turned. Several steps above Zee, she looked down from a commanding height. Not unlike a falcon, Zee thought, or a hawk. Wearing black leather head to toe.

"It's Zee. Do you remember me?"

"Of course I do. It's not everyone who bleeds all over my best Jinx & Jeremiah suede boots."

"Sorry. Can I talk to you for a second?" Even when Mia came down the steps to her level, she still towered over Zee. "I need to see David."

"He apparently didn't think so."

"I know. But I have to see him. One more time. Please, wherever he is, tell me. No matter where."

"They were putting together another research team, and he volunteered for it."

"Where?"

"He asked me not to tell you."

"Only because he thinks it's dangerous for me. You know that's the only reason."

As swiftly as if she were reaching for a gun, Mia reached into the pocket of her leather jacket, drew out a pen and notepad, and scribbled something on it. "I'm only doing this because I know he's miserable without you. But David's like a brother to me. If you put him in danger or harm him in any way—and I'm including a broken heart in that—I will find you and hurt you back. Just so you know."

"I would never hurt David," Zee answered. "I love him." She took the scrap of paper Mia handed her. "Prambanan? Where's that?"

"On Java, Indonesia. Bit of a religious war going on there. Hindus and Muslims. Should be fun. And you're still going, aren't you?"

Zee nodded.

"You two and your love," Mia said, turning to head back up the stairs. "You'll get us all killed."

CHAPTER THIRTEEN

HOME

*Z*ee tuned out the flight attendant's advice on steps to take in the event of an "unplanned structural breach" during the suborbital part of the flight. There wasn't much you *could* do in a .01 atmosphere, so what was the point? Besides, the trip had come together so much faster than Zee expected, she had plenty of other things to think about. Like what, exactly, would she say to David when she saw him? What if he really *didn't* want to see her ever again? What if he finished his research before she got there and returned to Omura, as Mia said he might?

These possibilities made a mere breach in the body

of the aircraft seem almost trivial. To calm herself, Zee touched the gold chain on her neck, with its decoration of three perfect diamonds. Or, more accurately, perfect faux diamonds.

Zee had gone first to her adviser in planning her trip. Since the burnout rate for empaths was high, Zee and her colleagues were encouraged to take breaks when needed, even on short notice, and were even given a small annual travel stipend. Zee had seldom used hers, and her adviser was delighted that she was at last going to. Colonel Dawson also pushed aside Zee's concerns about interrupting her training period.

"Prambanan!" he said, eyes lighting. "Damned fine choice! Mystical place, close to the spirit of things."

Until that moment, Zee had assumed that Prambanan was a city, or perhaps a suburb of Yogyakarta, where Jasmine lived. Colonel Dawson told her Prambanan was an eleven-hundred-year-old Buddhist temple, more or less in the middle of a jungle. Zee had spent the next several hours wondering how on Earth she'd get there until an email from Jasmine assured her it was only ten miles from Yogyakarta, with buses every hour.

Zee had dreaded telling Mrs. Hart most of all. She couldn't imagine leaving the older woman for weeks, even with her daughters and a barrage of home attendants looking after her.

"I won't go if you don't want me to," she volunteered.

"Don't be silly, dear." Mrs. Hart leaned forward and put her hand over Zee's. "I know you're afraid I'll shuffle off while you're gone, but you needn't be. Why, I wouldn't think of dying before I know how things turn out between you and your young man. And they *do* have a way of turning out, you know, no matter how bleak things may look. My life is proof of that. So you go ahead and follow your heart. I'll be around when you get back."

As she spoke, she unclasped the necklace she was wearing and poured the thin golden chain with its trio of diamonds into Zee's hand. "Take this for luck, Zee. It hasn't looked good on me for twenty-five years anyway. It needs a young throat. And young dreams."

"Oh, no, I couldn't—"

"Come, now, dear. Of course you can. They're only fakes, as you know. But my good wishes for you are real, and I'll feel better if I know it's with you."

So Zee had taken the necklace and now was glad Mrs. Hart had insisted. Each time she touched it, she remembered Mrs. Hart wishing her well.

Still, she was glad she wasn't going directly from London to Java. When she'd told her parents she was planning to visit Jasmine in Indonesia, it had taken no time at all to detect the disappointment in their voices. Realizing that they'd hoped she was calling to announce a trip home, Zee felt a pang of guilt mixed with true homesickness. "So I was wondering if I could stop and see you on my way," she added quickly. "It's been a long time since I was home."

It *had* been a long time. Almost two years, in fact, since she'd made the trip, as her family usually visited her in London. And when she arrived, it was a bit of a shock to find that the place she'd thought of all this time as home no longer felt like home to her. The house seemed large, after London spaces, and less cozy. Opening the door to her room, which she'd felt so sad to leave, was like stumbling into the room of a child she might once have known. It took her a minute to remember the music groups whose posters were on the walls.

"Why didn't you take this room when I moved out?" she asked her little sister. "It's bigger than yours."

"I know, but Mom said we had to keep it for you."

"Well, you don't have to keep it anymore. Why don't we fix it up for you while I'm here?"

Bex's eyes lit up. "Can we paint?"

"Sure. We can get paint tomorrow."

"But Mom and Dad—"

"Don't worry about Mom and Dad. I'll talk to them. It'll be okay." Zee grinned. "Start thinking of colors." Over the past year, Bex had lost her formless, bean-shaped look. Her legs were longer, and her bright red hair was growing darker and glossier, just as Zee's had at ten.

She waited until Bex went to bed to take up the subject with her parents. "It's just not fair to Bex," she began. "It's like you're telling her I deserve the room more, even though I'm not here,"

"But it's your room," her mother said. "What if you come back here to live? It would be like we'd gotten rid of you."

Zee didn't have the heart to tell her parents she was pretty sure her future, wherever it took her, didn't lie here. "If I come back," she said, "we'll do what we did when we were kids—we'll draw for it."

She saw that her parents weren't convinced. When had this started? They both acted like any change was a threat. Earlier, her father had told her that the neo-hippie group they'd been part of for so many years had fallen apart. No wonder he seemed at loose ends! Zee hadn't had many—any, really—boyfriends when she lived at home, and she'd been looking forward to telling them about David. She'd even thought that hearing how David had helped during the anarchists' attacks might restore some of her father's faith in the aliens. But he hadn't seemed to care one way or another.

"Why don't we make a family project of it, the way we used to?" she said. "I'm here three days, and if we all pitch in, we can switch the rooms and give Bex something really special."

And that's just what they did. Her father seemed to shake off all his disappointments and throw himself into creating a screen wall for Bex, who had turned into a techno geek and had now established a Worldwide Student News Network. Zee and her mother moved furniture while Bex tested various shades of illuminating blue paint on the walls.

"I want something that won't interfere with my glasses," she explained.

"Glasses?" Zee asked in surprise. No one had worn glasses for their eyesight for over 150 years. "Is that a new fad?"

"No, these," Bex said, handing Zee what looked like a gamer's headset with an extra large eye shield. "Try them on."

Zee did and her field of vision was instantly filled with about a hundred screens. "Eek! I feel like a fly! Help—how can I just look at one screen?"

Bex tapped the left rim of the visor a few times and the field reduced, showing only the upper right quadrant. "If you want to get to one screen, focus your view on the screen you want, or put on the gloves and you can touch your way to it."

"No thanks," said Zee, pulling the headset off. "I think I'll leave all of this sort of thing to you. What was I looking at, anyway?"

"Oh, those are just news stories I'm watching."

"I'm impressed," Zee said, and watched Bex glow.

They finished the room the night before Zee had to leave and celebrated with homemade pizza, creating crazy mosaics with the toppings just like they had when Zee was Bex's age.

Bex couldn't come to the vactrain station with them in the morning because she had an online editorial meeting, and Zee's father, who'd planned to drive, came down with a blinding migraine. In the end, it was just Zee and her mother waiting for the train.

"I hope Dad's okay," Zee fretted.

"He will be. He just can't stand to see you go is all. He really loved having you here. And you were great with him, Zee. Lately he's been so—"

"I know. Mom, did you see what a great job he did on the work in Bex's room? Those built-ins he made? That kind of workmanship is pretty hard to find. Maybe now that the neo-hippies have disbanded . . . well, I bet lots of people around here would hire him to do custom work like that."

"What a great idea, Zee." Her mother paused. "I wish we saw more of you. You've grown up so much in the last year, and now you're off to see that boy."

Zee's eye opened wide. "You know?"

"Well, not for sure. Not until just now. But I had a hunch. Indonesia is a long way to go just to see Jasmine. And so suddenly. It's that boy who took you out for your birthday, isn't it? And helped during the bomb attacks? Don't look so surprised. Every mother started out as a girl in love, you know, even me."

"I wish you could meet him, but everything's so uncertain. He transferred to Indonesia because he doesn't think we should see each other anymore, since his time here is almost up and he has to go back to his home planet."

"And you're going to talk him out of it?"

"I—I don't know. I only know I have to see him one more time. I have to make sure it's what *he* wants to do, not something he's doing to try to protect me." She stopped abruptly and studied her mother's face. "Do you think I'm stupid for doing this? I mean, I know I've never had a boyfriend before, so it must seem like I've gone totally off the deep end and—"

Her mother gave her a quick, hard hug. The rumbling vibrations under their feet signaled the imminent arrival of the vactrain. "I don't think you're off the deep end, Zee. You could have had tons of boyfriends by now, but you always had other things on your mind. So if this boy has your heart, he must be special. And I'd hate to see you go through life without having that. You'd better go now, or you'll miss that train. And don't worry about your father. We'll be fine."

"Bye, Mom. I'll email when I get there. Love you." Hugging her mother good-bye, Zee noticed for the first time that she was now the taller of the two of them.

CHAPTER FOURTEEN

THE GREEN BUDDHA

The closer Zee had gotten, the more her doubts grew. It had been one thing to stand on the familiar vactrain platform at home and set off for parts unknown. It was another thing to actually *be* in parts unknown, on a mission that seemed increasingly uncertain. If David had truly cared about her, wouldn't he have stayed? There were many moments, high over the Pacific, when her palm would close around the Neptune's Tears necklace and she would hear Mrs. Hart's voice telling her to follow her heart.

Jasmine and her boyfriend, Rajasa, met Zee at the airport, though how they found her in the shoulder-to-shoulder sea of people, Zee would never know. Rajasa—Raj for short—was as attractive as the hologram Jasmine had sent and charming to boot. He even managed to get them a seat on an airbus so crowded that several passengers had to get off before it could even leave the ground.

"Is it rush hour already?" Zee asked, and Raj and Jasmine laughed.

"It's always like this," Jasmine explained. "Except on holidays—"

"When it's much worse," Raj finished. They looked at each other and smiled over the joke they'd shared many times.

Jasmine's apartment was tiny, barely as big as Zee's two rooms in the residence hall. *But*, Jasmine told her, larger than anything most couples could afford.

"Couples?" Zee's eyebrows lifted.

"You're the first to know," said Raj with a huge grin. "I've asked Princess Jasmine to marry me, and she said yes. I have no idea why."

"Because you are so rich," Jasmine teased, "And I promised Mama I would marry a rich businessman."

Raj had just started his residency at the hospital where Jasmine worked as an empath. They would be broke for years, and both would earn less than they would have elsewhere, but neither seemed to mind. In this lush, crowded country of a thousand tiny islands, they had found each other, and that was what mattered. Jasmine, who'd been plump and worn layers of clothes against the cold even in the middle of England's summer, had blossomed like an exotic flower since Zee had last seen her. She'd grown thinner—"No chips! No more jelly doughnuts!"—and lost the shadow of something Zee had seen in herself, in David, and even in confident Mia—homesickness. She and Raj would live their lives where they were born. Their children would grow up with grandparents and cousins. Their work and their lives would make their country stronger, and their contentment with all of this shed light like a small sun. Zee thought of her time with David and how almost every minute seemed to have been danced on a tightrope. It was hard not to envy Jasmine and Raj, or what it would be like to be them.

After Raj left, Zee told Jasmine about David, leaving out, as she had for her parents, Omura's nasty habit of destroying one or both partners if the relationship was discovered.

"And you came all this way to surprise him!" Jasmine sighed. "It's so romantic! I can't wait to meet him."

"One thing at a time," Zee said. "I mean, what if he doesn't want to see me?"

"Why wouldn't he want to see you? Of *course* he'll want to see you."

It had been nice to hear, even if Zee herself was having doubts. The next day, she went to Prambanan and found she'd been there almost three hours without having made her way to the building where David was working. Part of it was procrastination, she knew, but part of it was Prambanan itself. She'd been so caught up in the idea of finding David, she hadn't given a thought to what a Hindu temple might look like.

She'd arrived early in the morning, when the mists were still clearing. As the fog lifted, the central temples came into view, each one shaped like a torch with spiky points reaching into the sky. Getting off the bus and starting down the broad avenue that led to the central plaza, she saw other temples. Not just one or two or even a few dozen but hundreds of them, some as tall as a house, some barely as tall as she was, some empty, some housing statues of Hindu gods and goddesses, some perfectly intact, and some mysteriously toppled into ruins. But what amazed her, when she got to the large buildings, were the relief sculptures carved into the stone walls. On almost every building, panel after panel of men and women danced out stories of love, faith, and passion. Each figure was so carefully carved, with an expression so different from all the others, that

Zee could have recognized each of them in a crowd. They were portraits of people who had lived over thirteen hundred years ago, yet their expressions so perfectly echoed her own hope and despair that she felt bound to them, another dancer in the endless chain.

<hr />

He had tried every way he knew to forget her. When the opportunity to transfer to the Prambanan research team came up, he volunteered immediately and spent the rest of the afternoon feeling like he'd cut off his own arm. To board the plane, he'd told himself a fantasy about returning to London in a few weeks and watching her from afar without letting her know.

He wasn't even sure why he loved her, except that when he was with her, he felt like someone he'd always wanted to be. He didn't feel the weight of his family's expectations for him, didn't feel he was trying to find the right words to impress someone who would forever remain a mystery to him. There was no mystery with Zee. She was home to him, and he knew they were meant to be together.

Only they couldn't be. He'd lied to her, over and over again. Lied about who he was and why he was here, and he would never be able to tell her the truth.

She who was so strong and yet so vulnerable, who had used all of her spending money to buy him the eagle talisman, then been too shy to give it to him. He would never forgive himself for failing to protect her from the cruel truths that engulfed them, truths she was not even aware of. He had no right to interfere with her life more than he already had.

Yet even this far away, she filled the space around him. The drifting scent of flowers and citrus reminded him of her. When the wind changed and brought the warm, humid sea air inland, he thought of their day at Brighton and the way they'd kissed at the edge of the dark sea. The voices of American tourists that drifted to him as he worked were so like hers he would put down what he was doing and listen, willing it to be her. And so one day when he left the small, sweltering manuscript room he was working in to take a break and saw, down one of the long grassy alleys between the miniature temples, a girl with lush red hair standing with her back to him, it made all the sense in the world that it would be Zee.

* * *

She had almost decided to go back to Jasmine's and postpone seeing him until tomorrow. Her emotions were tangled, and she still had jet lag. But suddenly, she felt the warmth of him and the call of his thoughts all around her, and turned to see him standing there.

"Zee?"

She had rehearsed a hundred things to say, from love to anger. But now, face-to-face, she had no words at all. They stood staring until he reached for her, wrapping her in his arms and holding her tight. "I know," he whispered. "I know."

Later, she would never remember exactly what they said to each other, or what was said with words and what was said without. She remembered that once they touched each other, they did not let go and that in his embrace she felt, as she had so often before, the turmoil that held him tighter than she ever could.

At some point, she must have asked him how he could have left her the way he did, without a note and without intending to come back, because she remembered him saying, "It was the only way I could leave you at all, Zee. And staying would have been too dangerous, even with Mia helping us. It would have put you both in danger. So I thought if I left that way, you might be angry enough to forget me."

They spent the rest of the afternoon together wandering among the temples. He showed her his favorite structures and sometimes told her the meanings of the relief carvings. Transcribing them into words was part of the research he was doing, and he knew the stories well. According to legend, the many temples of Prambanan had been built in a single night by a prince to win the heart of a beautiful young woman.

"And did he?" Zee asked.

David shook his head. "No. Even after he fulfilled her challenge, she still refused to marry him. So great was her cruel indifference that the gods turned her into a serpent."

"Seems fair," Zee said, and they tightened their arms around each other.

At the end of the afternoon, as he walked her to the buses at the visitor's center, he turned suddenly quiet. "What do we do now, Zee? Nothing has changed, you know, no matter how we feel about each other. Omura still is going to make me come back. I have another two months of work here, and my Earth time runs out a few months after that. If I'm not on a ship back, they'll come looking for me. And they might find you. It's too dangerous to keep seeing each other in London. I'm planning to request a straight home rotation from here."

The enormity of their situation washed over Zee. If it was truly as hopeless as he said . . .

"Shouldn't we at least have this?" she asked at last. "If this is all we have, shouldn't we take it? We can pretend we're just two ordinary people. We can have more days like today. Isn't that better than nothing at all?"

In the end, that's just what they did. Through an effort of imagination and will, they managed to forget their circumstances and have this perfect time together. Some days Zee shopped for lunch in town, then hopped on the bus to Prambanan and surprised him with a picnic. On Jasmine's day off, Zee toured the local arts and crafts market with her, buying presents for her family, Rani, Mrs. Hart, her adviser, and even Colonel Dawson.

"How is Rani?" Jasmine asked as Zee paid for the handmade sandals with peacock blue crystals that would suit Rani's narrow, high-arched feet to a tee.

"You know our Rani." Zee laughed. "Breaking hearts left and right, determined never to succumb herself."

At sunset, David bicycled into town to spend the evenings with Zee. Often they ate dinner with Jasmine and Raj, all four of them cooking, laughing, and washing up in Jasmine's tiny kitchen sink. One evening, Raj urged them to hurry through the meal so they could take in a real Indonesian specialty, a neighborhood badminton contest.

David confessed he'd never seen badminton played at all. To Zee it was a lazy game played on summer holidays like the Fourth of July. Both of them were un-prepared for the huge crowd that had gathered in an empty lot between large apartment buildings. There were even vendors selling flavored ices and sweets.

"There must be three hundred people here," David said.

"Just wait until the game *really* gets going," Raj promised. Two neighborhoods with a longstanding rivalry were going up against each other. As the weaker seeds played each other, more and more people continued to arrive. When Zee looked up, she could see people watching from apartment balconies and crowded windows. There were even people lining the roofs. It was stifling in the crowd, but the heat seemed only to increase the tension and excitement. With each round, the contestants became better and better, playing a game nothing like the lazy, lackadaisical pastime Zee knew. The shuttlecock flew back and forth with amazing speed. Players rarely missed making a return shot, giving their rackets so much power that the swoop of air through racket strings and resounding *thwunk* of the shuttlecock could be heard throughout the crowd. As the long summer evening grew dark, people brought old-fashioned electric lamps out to light the court, connected to outlets by extension cords that trailed out of apartment windows. By the time the top players faced off against each other, the crowd was charged with excitement. Every returned volley was cheered, and every missed shot got a gasp of despair. It was past one in the morning, and the noise was deafening.

"Aren't they afraid the neighbors will complain?" Zee asked.

Jasmine laughed. "There's no one to complain. Everyone's here."

The final sets were the best, so fraught with tension Zee couldn't look away, her eyes so focused on the flying shuttlecock she felt the image was permanently burned onto her retinas.

By the time the final winners received their rounds of applause, the crowd was limp with exhaustion. "I guess we'll know who to watch for in the next Olympics," Zee commented.

Raj shrugged. "These are just the neighborhood best. Not even close to making the Olympic team."

The next night, David arrived with a set of borrowed rackets and a canister of shuttlecocks, and he and Zee set off for a park to try their hand. They were both miserable at it, and counted it a great success to keep the shuttlecock in the air for more than a minute at a time. Two of the shuttlecocks they lost in the shrubs, though Zee found one of them later and quietly tucked it into her pocket to keep. For a split second, she remembered that she was leaving in a few days, and a sadness close to panic rose within her. Then she returned to David, smiling as best she could.

Walking back to Jasmine's, David asked her if there was anything special she wanted to do on her last day.

"Not really," Zee said. The very words *last day* sounded like a death sentence.

"Good," David said, "because there's someplace special I want you to see. We'll have to leave here about four in the morning to catch it, though. Are you up for it?"

Zee nodded. "Are you going to tell me what it is?"

"No way," David said. "It's a surprise. But I'm renting a car, so I promise to get you to the airport in plenty of time for your flight."

Zee packed the night before, and because she'd be gone by the time Jasmine woke up, she placed the gift she'd bought for her on the table. It was a beautifully embroidered bed coverlet worked in Jasmine's favorite colors of blues and greens. Vines ran along the borders, making a home for swallows that took flight across the coverlet's center. Slipping away to buy it the day Jasmine took her to the art market hadn't been easy, but Zee was sure she'd kept the purchase a secret, and smiled to think of Jasmine's surprise. She'd just finished tucking a note into the wrappings when she heard soft footsteps on the stairs, and opened the door before David could knock. As he started downstairs with her single piece of luggage, she took a final look around the apartment. *Happy life, Jasmine. Happy, happy life.* Then she closed the door softly and hurried to follow her own fate.

⁕+ ⸙ ⁕+⁹

The sky had just begun to lighten when they arrived, though sunrise itself was still half an hour away. The visitor's center wasn't open yet, but there was a light on inside. David went around to the back and returned minutes later with two passes and a parking sticker. "I worked here a few days before Prambanan," he explained as he tethered the car securely. Like all cars on Java, it was an older model, one of the first pneumatics that had come along, but that didn't mean it couldn't be stolen. He held his hand out to Zee. "Let's go."

She still couldn't see anything but dark jungle falling away on all sides. "Where are we?"

"This is Borobudur," he explained, "the largest Buddhist temple on Java. It was built about the same time Prambanan was, over a millennium ago. Both temples were partially destroyed by an earthquake and this whole area was abandoned. When explorers stumbled on them in the seventeenth century, no one knew they'd ever existed."

Zee thought of the portrait sculptures on the walls of Prambanan, dancing in silence as the jungle grew towards them, their faces and the names of those who'd imagined them forgotten. Was that what life was? You lived, you danced, you were forgotten? No, she thought with sudden insight. Others found you. Explorers came along and found you. People like David retrieved your story. Nothing you did was ever truly lost.

"Can you see it?" David was asking.

Zee squinted at what seemed a gathering of shadows in the distance. As they walked closer, she saw that it was a large building, built in tiers of dark stone. The tiers were cracked and uneven. Whole sections seemed to tilt. Compared to Prambanan with its grassy paths and tiny temples, Borobudur seemed unfriendly, almost menacing.

"What's inside, then?" she asked.

"Nothing. This is solid stone."

The grounds weren't open yet, and so they were the only people on the path that led to the vast, eerie structure. The only sound was the occasional screech of a monkey. She wondered why he'd brought her here but said nothing.

As if reading her thoughts, David paused when they came near the foot of the monument. "Do you see them now?"

At first she didn't, but then suddenly, despite the dim murkiness, she did. Looking out at them from every tier, from corners and alcoves and parapets, were Buddhas, hundreds of them. Their serenity transformed everything around them.

"Ready to climb, then?" he asked.

"You mean we can go up to them?"

"Sure, all the way to the top. Follow me."

On her own, Zee could have spent hours on each tier, examining the statues and taking in the patterns carved into the stones. She noticed that while all the Buddhas were seated in a lotus position, their hands were in many different poses. Some held their hands palm to palm in prayer, some touched the Earth, some held objects, some rested one hand on a knee and raised the other to visitors in peace. She wanted to slow down and count the possibilities, but David was a man with a mission and kept urging her upward.

"Perfect," he said when they reached the large, square top.

The first thing Zee saw was structures shaped like old-fashioned handbells, the kind town criers rang, only they were made of stone and brick and much taller than a human. Through their many small, diamond-shaped openings, Zee saw that each contained a Buddha, and more Buddhas sat in low stone circles looking out toward the horizon.

"We're just in time," David said. He led her quickly to the east-facing wall, and Zee gasped at the view. Far below them lay the dense jungle, deep green with a canopy of fog drifting just above it. The green reflected up through the fog to give everything a soft green glow, even the pale stone Buddha who kept watch with them. If Zee hadn't known better, she would have sworn the statue was carved of the palest milky jade. As she watched, the sun broke above the horizon. In an instant, its rays transformed the Buddha to shimmering gold. The effect lasted no more than a minute, but Zee would never forget its magic.

"This is my favorite Buddha of all," she said.

"Mine too, and there's no one I'd want to share him with but you. Here." He reached into his pocket and pulled out a square of folded tissue paper. "Sorry there's no box. They're not big on gift wrap here."

Zee unfolded the square of tissue to discover a thin gold bracelet with two Buddhas on it, one pale jade and the second, smaller figure pure, heavy gold. "Oh," she breathed, "they're wonderful. I'm never going to take it off."

She handed him the chain and extended her wrist. When his fingertips brushed against the soft skin of her inner wrist, she shivered, never wanting the moment to end. She felt him tremble against her and knew he felt the same.

But the moment was ending, she saw. The Buddha—*their* Buddha—was mellowing to the tawny glow of morning. Soon it would be time to leave for the airport.

"What does it mean when their hands are in different positions?" she asked. "Why is ours touching the ground with one hand?"

"The hands express different aspects of the Buddha's teachings. Our touch-the-earth Buddha signifies calling the Earth to witness."

"Then," Zee said, "I call the Earth to witness that this has been the best week of my entire life."

"Mine too," David said, looking directly into her eyes. "I wish we could do it all again."

"But we can," Zee said. "Come back to London. Something might change. You never know. And if it doesn't, at least we can be together a little while longer."

David's mouth turned suddenly hard. "Yes, something might happen. We might get caught."

"But we've been lucky so far. Why wouldn't we be again?"

He folded her in his arms. "I'd do anything to be

with you, Zee. But you don't know what it's like if they catch you."

"Yes I do," she said stubbornly, an edge in her voice. "You told me all about it."

"But it's not real to you. I've seen them rip couples apart, one to prison, one to oblivion. I can't let that happen to you."

"Promise me you'll think about coming back to London. Promise me just that much."

He said nothing, and they stood there silently holding each other for a long time, until the first of the day's tourists reached the top of the monument and they surrendered the spot on Earth where they'd been the happiest.

CHAPTER FIFTEEN

SHUTTLECOCK

Four nights in a row, Zee dreamt about the shuttlecock. The dreams began just after she returned to London, and at first she thought nothing of them. She was thinking about David all the time. She was emotionally exhausted. Watching the neighborhood games, then trying to play badminton with David the next day, had been high points of her trip, so it wasn't surprising that her subconscious would try to keep the trip going. And it wasn't surprising that the shuttlecock was the shorthand her dreaming mind chose. The shuttlecock she and David had lost and she'd found later was sitting on her table. More than once she found herself sketching it, halfway through before she even realized it.

Zee mentioned this to Colonel Dawson when she gave him the present she'd bought in the art market. She was eager to pick up where she'd left off, but wondered if the dreams would interfere.

"Sometimes traveling, particularly to a place so out of one's usual orbit, so to speak, stirs things up. Have you ever had clairvoyant dreams before?"

"No. I've had a lot of catastrophe dreams—sandstorms and cyclones, war, people I know being stabbed. But none of them ever happened."

"Well, then, this probably means nothing at all. But I'm wondering if you'd do me a personal favor. Would you mind taking a few more tests for me? It's for a theory I'm exploring, on whether certain experiences and destinations can affect highly intuitive people. Especially someone young like yourself, who's in the midst of—" He broke off suddenly.

"In the midst of what?"

"Sorry," said the colonel. "None of my business."

"Please tell me what you were going to say."

"Just that you seem to be in the midst of a transition."

"Transition? To what?"

"Ah, that I wouldn't know. But you seem different since you went away. Now"—he picked up the gift she'd wrapped in colored paper and tied with ribbon— "what do we have here?"

It wasn't an expensive gift, just a small handwoven basket with a lid, but the colonel was delighted. "It's going right on my desk," he said.

Bringing home gifts was definitely one of the best parts of traveling, Zee thought. Rani had loved her sandals with the peacock blue crystals, and the silk shawl she took to Mrs. Hart had softened Zee's awareness that her friend was now confined to bed and close to the end of her long life.

The second set of tests the colonel gave her was more complex than the first, laying out specific scenarios that involved more people than objects or locations. Though the tests were much more detailed and the colonel pressed her to home in on her answers and make them more specific, Zee didn't necessarily find them harder. At the end, he once again brought out his miniature theater, the one that had fascinated and defeated Zee the first time around. This time, however, she had a far easier time assessing the people inside the box.

After Zee had correctly identified the culprit in two

crime cases and the victim in an attempted kidnapping, the colonel asked her to wear a headband with sensors connected to the theater's motherboard. Zee realized this was exactly the situation she'd feared when the over-enthusiastic Dr. Branning had suggested it. But Colonel Dawson wasn't Dr. Branning, and Zee was no longer afraid. She was curious and eager to see where her improved accuracy would lead.

Headband in place, Zee watched the miniature figures inside the transparent box. This time, the minute she identified the culprit, he vanished.

"Keep watching," the Colonel said.

Zee did, and over the next several minutes was able to identify two accomplices she'd initially missed.

"Wow."

"Wow indeed. You're deepening, Zee. You have great potential to be a top diviner. You've already had some experience with the anarchists at Blackfriars Bridge. I'd like to put you specifically to work with the anarchist threat team I'm in charge of. Interested?"

"Yes." Nothing would be more satisfying, she thought, than stopping the fear and suffering caused by shock bombs.

"I have to warn you that, as a novice, your input won't have as much weight as more experienced people on the team. But here's a card with my private number, always with me and always on. If you ever have an overwhelming feeling about something, call me. Especially over the next few months."

"Is there a particular threat, then?"

The colonel chuckled and indicated a screen scrolling continuous data. "Twenty thousand of them. Almost twice the daily load."

On the way home, Zee realized that her assertion about her disastrous dreams never happening wasn't completely true. *Sandstorms and cyclones, war, people I know being stabbed.* . . . Hadn't David been stabbed? And she herself? But the dream she'd had was long ago, before she'd even come to London. In the dream, her sister, Bex, was grown up and married to a man who traveled a lot for his work, and he was stabbed on a flight coming home. Zee recalled having read that when dreams held troubling thoughts, the dreamer often chose a stand-in for themselves. But even if Bex had been a stand-in, it wouldn't explain the rest of the dream. She hadn't known David then, so she couldn't very well have dreamt about him. Like most dreams, it was probably a random collection of worries, incidents, and images from her day. And since there were only so many images and incidents that could occur, it wasn't surprising that dreams and reality should mirror each other from time to time.

When the dreams started up again, she thought it might be more than just jet lag. In the first set of dreams, there was nothing unusual about the shuttle- cock. Small and white, it flew back and forth in a game where she was a contestant. The second set of dreams was different. The shuttlecock was larger, and instead of stiff little white feathers, it trailed long, brilliantly col- ored plumes. In this version of the dream, Zee was only a spectator. It was Rani who held the racket, though Zee couldn't see who she was playing with. Midway through each dream, the shuttlecock would turn and fly away, and Rani would float after it, laughing and sometimes glancing back over her shoulder at Zee.

This time, Zee knew Rani was a substitute for herself, and the shuttlecock was meant to be David— bright, alluring, the thing she would follow after. The thing that would not go the way she expected but would always fly away from her.

Because that was exactly what was happening. Her first days back in London had been easy. She knew David was finishing his research in Prambanan. But as time passed, she knew David would be leaving there. She began expecting to see him each time she turned a corner and with every breath she took. It was inconceivable that he wouldn't come back to London, unimaginable that he would return to Omura without seeing her again. But she knew too that it wasn't her decision to make. It was David's, and whatever he did would become part of her life. Seen that way, the dreams made all the sense in the world. Even so, she'd learned her lesson from the tsunami. She wrote a detailed report on the shuttlecock dreams for Colonel Dawson, emphasizing their growing intensity and the way various parts grew more brilliant and elaborate with each new dream. Last night, the feathered tips had turned fiery orange and burst into flame.

The call she'd been dreading came on a Tuesday afternoon, just as she finished writing her notes on a young man who'd come back from the Mars colony with a bad case of space pleurisy. When Zee heard the voice of Mrs. Hart's daughter, she stiffened, afraid she'd already missed a chance to say good-bye. But that was why she was calling. Mrs. Hart wanted to know if Zee could "pop round" as soon as possible. Zee knew exactly what that meant but smiled despite herself. It was just like Ellie Hart to use a jaunty phrase like *pop round.*

Zee found her friend propped in bed, wearing the

silk shawl Zee had given her. She looked, Zee thought, carefree in the true sense of the word—free of care.

"Bring a chair over by the bed, will you, Zee? I don't have the strength to project across the room. I must say, this shawl is a fine thing to make an exit in. Much better dressed than when I arrived." She caught the uncertain look in Zee's eye. "Oh, please, let there be laughter, Zee, even if my joke wasn't a very good one. You can't take death too seriously, not at my age. You know, when I was your age, death was much more common. Few people lived beyond eighty or ninety. It was part of everyone's experience, and people were much less fearful of it. I'm not sure extending life so long has done humanity any favors. It's made people forget what life is for."

"What *is* life for, then?"

"Well, it's a matter of opinion, of course, but I think it's for learning. Learning to love each other, leaving things better than we found them."

Zee thought of the five hundred statues of Buddha at Borobudur, how they were all different yet all serene in their expressions of wisdom and compassion. Maybe that was what her life was meant to be. It had been weeks, and there had been no word from David. Maybe her life was to be one of helping others and never knowing love herself. But it was hard, when you were seventeen and wanted so much to be loved and to have a future like everyone else's.

She must have uttered these thoughts aloud, for the silence was broken when Mrs. Hart said, "Ah. No word from the young man, then?"

"No."

"Well, it's not over until it's over."

Mrs. Hart closed her eyes and seemed to drift off. Zee was content to sit quietly beside her. There was a profound, almost luminous, sense of peace in the room. Maybe Mrs. Hart was right—it wasn't over until it was over.

Zee didn't know how long they sat like that. Time seemed to be moving rapidly, but the sun was still bright when Mrs. Hart opened her eyes again.

"Sorry I dozed off, dear. Where was I? Oh, yes, life. Big topic, isn't it?" She closed her eyes again and was quiet for so long Zee thought she'd dozed off again. Then suddenly, her hand tightened over Zee's. "And you've been one of the nice surprises of my life, Zee. When you live this long, you think you've had everything you're going to get. But knowing you has been a delight. You're very special, and all the dearer because you don't know how special you are."

Zee had promised herself she wouldn't cry in front of Mrs. Hart, but suddenly, she felt the sting of tears behind her eyes.

"I'm going to miss you so much!" she said.

"Oh, you'll hear from me from time to time. I'll be around. Just a small change of address. And, Zee? No matter what happens, be bold with your life. Don't settle for small. When your heart tells you something's right, go big. Risk it all. *That's* what life is really for."

CHAPTER SIXTEEN

THE FIRES OF MONTGOLFIER

It had been a week since Mrs. Hart's funeral, meaning it was more than two months since Zee had left Indonesia. Where was David? There'd been no word from him, and even her attempts to find Mia proved futile. The expectation of seeing David walking down the street toward her left a dull, ever-present ache in her chest. Sometimes the thought of living the rest of her life without ever seeing him again rose in her mind, but she would push it swiftly away. As Mrs. Hart had said, it wasn't over until it was over. And for Zee it wasn't over. Maybe it never would be. Maybe she would go her whole life loving only him.

"You poor baby," Rani said. "I can't believe this is the first time you've been in love."

"You mean you've been in love before?"

"I'm in love every day," Rani said. "I love Josh's smile and Ian's blue eyes. I love it that Sanjay is Hindu like me so I never have to explain being a vegetarian. I love Caleb because he's a brainiac but kind of goofy too."

"It isn't the same," Zee said.

"I know." She shrugged. "Maybe someday. Oh—did you check your mail today? The French are invading Cornwall for Bastille Day. Some sort of huge fair. And because of that seminar we did in Paris, we're invited as special guests. Listen to this." Rani pulled out her invitation and read. "Party like it's 1789! Join us in Cornwall for a day of traditional food and fun worthy of Marie-Antoinette herself. Amusements include *la Comédie-Française, jeux de hasard, danses traditionnelles, pantomimes, jongleurs, et montgolfières fantastiques.* Doesn't it sound thrilling?"

"Rani, do you know what even half of those words mean?"

"No, but I'm sure they're fun. A week from Saturday, and it's all free. They even sent us vactrain passes." She paused, caught by Zee's expression. "Oh, no. Oh, no, don't tell me you're even *thinking* of not going."

"I'm sorry, Rani. I just don't think I feel like traipsing across England right now."

"But you've never been to Cornwall! It's beautiful. You can't say you've truly lived in England if you haven't been to Cornwall. And you can't stay cooped up here forever."

"I know, but—"

"But nothing," Rani said. "You have to come. We've been specially invited."

"I can't," Zee said. What if she went, and David showed up after all, and she wasn't here to see him?

"Okay," Rani said. "If you're not going, then neither am I."

"But you're looking forward to it!"

"Yes, but if you're not up to going, you certainly aren't up to being left alone. I'm not leaving you here to mope on your own."

Zee sighed. Rani knew her like she knew herself and used it to her advantage. Certain that Zee would never make her miss the festivities, she played it to the hilt.

"All right," she said at last. "I'll go."

"You might even meet someone there." Rani smiled. "After all, you never know what the future holds."

They planned to leave early for the fair, and Zee was up and dressed when Rani knocked softly at seven A.M. When the door swung open, she gasped. Rani seldom wore a sari unless she was going to a family wedding or celebration. This morning she was not only wearing traditional clothes but was dressed in the most beautiful sari Zee had ever seen, saffron colored with an intricately patterned border in a hundred shades of orange and crimson. She wore gold bracelets on both wrists and on her feet the blue-crystal-embellished sandals Zee had brought her.

In jeans and a T-shirt, Rani was a pretty, mischievous girl with dancing eyes. In a sari, she was a breathtaking beauty, the image of her great-great-grandmother, the Bollywood star.

"Rani! You look like a princess!"

"It's the oddest thing," Rani explained as they headed for the train station. "I was going to wear my usual, when I heard Great-great-grandmother Nalini telling me to wear this sari. Isn't that weird? But you never ignored what Nalini said, so here I am." Rani laughed. "Who knows? Maybe I'm meant to meet a handsome Hindu prince!"

Rani had been right that Cornwall was beautiful. When they emerged from the vactrain, they boarded a bus that took them up into the giant hills that bordered the ocean and fell away to the sea. The air was clear and bright with sunlight that sparkled like diamonds on the water below. The hilltop was covered with booths and stands manned by people in peasant garb while gorgeously dressed members like the soon-to-fall aristocracy strolled the wide grassy lawn. Rani, in her saffron-colored sari, looked oddly at home next to the pink, pale blue, and yellow satins of the old order.

They strolled from booth to booth, enjoying the jugglers and trying to decide what to eat. They'd just agreed on crepes with fresh strawberries when Rani spotted a booth that was making chocolates as they had before the Revolution, pressing small molds into a tray of powdered sugar, then removing the molds and pouring melted chocolate into the indentations.

As they walked, Rani kept looking over the crowd.

"Looking for that Indian prince?" Zee teased.

"Something like that," Rani said.

Finally, they settled on the strawberry crepes and found space at one of the tables decorated with red, white, and blue cockades and small French flags. With the warm July sun falling on her and the taste of sweetness and strawberries in her mouth, the world seemed almost hopeful again.

"Thanks for making me come, Rani," Zee said. "I guess you're right. Life does go on."

But Rani didn't seem to be listening. "Oh my gosh, there's Lucy Willis," she said, staring across the crowd. "We were best friends in primary school. I can't believe it. Do you mind if I say hello? I'll be back in just a second."

Zee motioned her to go and went back to her crepe. She hadn't had such an appetite in weeks, and contemplated finishing Rani's crepe if she didn't return soon.

"Excuse me, is this seat taken?"

Zee froze, knowing why and not knowing in the same instant. She looked up. *Him.* Her David, with his gray eyes and straight black eyebrows. Nothing in her life had ever felt as wonderful as the moment when their arms went around each other once again. She pressed her face against his chest and inhaled deeply, taking in his scent, his warmth, and his love for her. In that single breath, her entire world expanded.

"I thought I'd never see you again. I thought—" She stopped, the salt of her own trickling tears in her mouth.

"Ssh, ssh, Zee." When he kissed her, she tasted like fresh air and strawberries. The day would still come when he would have to give her up, but after she left Prambanan, he realized what she'd known all along—that every day they could be together would be one of the best days of their lives.

She pulled her head back and for an endless moment, they stood like that, looking into each other's eyes. "For as long as we have, then," she said at last, and he realized her fierce courage was greater than his own.

Not long after that, Rani came up to them. "See?" She beamed. "I told you you might meet someone. I just didn't say who."

"You knew about this?"

"Of course I did. And now that I've done my duty for true love, there's a cute guy named Étienne over there who's promised me an absolutely thrilling ride in his *montgolfière*, so I'll catch up with you later."

There it was again, that funny French word that had been in the invitation, *montgolfière*. It must be a kind of airscooter, Zee thought, or an antique car. "Be careful," she called after Rani. "You know what your mother would say about riding in fast cars with strange boys."

Rani looked back at Zee and laughed. "Of course. But she's said nothing about riding in strange cars with fast boys!" The musical notes of her laugh were torn and carried by the wind, and the last Zee heard from her as she vanished into the crowd.

David was looking a little chagrined. "I hope you

don't think I put Rani in danger," he said, "but they're still monitoring me, so I needed a place where we could meet in public, and I needed a way of making sure you'd be here."

"Won't they wonder why you're here on your own, though?"

"Oh, I'm not alone. Mia's floating around here somewhere. With a new boyfriend, of course. Really, she and Rani are two of a kind."

They spent the next hour drifting around the fair, then found a grassy spot looking out over the water and sat, leaning against each other in the warm sun. Suddenly, David felt Zee's muscles go tight against him. She leapt to her feet and stood trembling.

"Zee, what is it?"

A large hot-air balloon had come into view several miles south and appeared to be coming toward them. A second soon followed, then a third. Silhouetted against the sun, Zee saw it clearly—the inverted tear-drop shape of each balloon, the passenger gondola below it, and the fretwork of cables that tethered the two together perfectly mimicked a shuttlecock.

David was on his feet too, putting a calming hand on her shoulder. "It's okay, Zee. They're just hot-air balloons."

"In French," she said. "What are they called in French?"

"*Montgolfières.*"

Zee went rigid with fear. She realized now that her dreams had been a series of warnings—warnings she had once again failed to interpret correctly. And because she'd failed, they were now all in danger. And Rani—lovely, lively Rani—she feared was in the most danger of all.

"There's going to be an anarchist attack," she said. "From one of those balloons. Go find a policeman or a security guard and bring him back here as quickly as you can. Drag him, if you have to."

While David was gone, Zee called Colonel Dawson and told him what was happening. "We have to stop them. Are there any MI5 agents here?"

"No," the colonel said. "No, they've been spread very thin lately."

"Then we have to stop them ourselves. Can you help us, colonel?

Everything that happened next seemed to take hours to unfold. In reality, events took little more than an hour, a fact that would forever confound Zee.

David had located a policeman and explained the situation, but his demands for proof were so loud

Colonel Dawson must have heard them over the phone. "Ask him if he's ever heard of suicide by brain implosion," the colonel said. "Tell him he's about to talk to the man who invented it."

Once the policeman was on board, step one was to order an immediate halt to further balloon launches. Then they found a car and drove the few short miles to the launch site. None of the four balloons remaining on the ground looked like the one in her dream or triggered a response in Zee, which meant they would have to go aloft and try to identify and chase down the threat.

"One thing you all need to know," the colonel said. "We don't think this is a standard shock bomb. The threat assessment team thinks it's biochemical and nearly 100 percent lethal. If it's released over that crowd, almost everyone directly below will die within a few hours. That means it's lethal to you as well. This is strictly a volunteer mission. No one will think less of you for bowing out."

Zee, David, the policeman, and the balloon pilot who'd agreed to take them up looked at each other.

"I'm the only one who can identify the balloon," Zee told David. "But you don't have to go. Stay here and wait. I'll be okay."

David took her hand. "You're not going alone."

Finally, the pilot said, "Let's do it, then."

Despite the fact that the balloon was equipped with air jets and a modern steering mechanism, they rose with maddening slowness. As they did, Zee tried to look down into the gondolas of the grounded balloons. Was Rani in one of them? There hadn't been time to find out. Every minute they lost brought all of them, and the hundreds of people at the fair, closer to death.

When the balloon rose to the top of the cliffs, they could see six other balloons. Two Zee had already seen and ruled out. That left four. She handed her phone to David, who took over relaying the colonel's directions to the others. Zee closed her eyes and cleared her mind. She saw again the balloon in her dreams, its brilliant colors and intricate patterns. When she opened her eyes, the pilot had brought them much closer to the other balloons, and Zee knew at once which balloon it was. She also knew it was the balloon Rani was in, for even at this distance she could see an edge of her saffron sari fluttering in the wind. *Oh, Rani, why, just this once, couldn't you have said no to the exciting boy offering you a ride?* Quietly, Zee reached for the edge of the gondola and gripped the rail to steady herself.

The colonel's plan was for the pilot to maneuver their balloon between the anarchist's and the crowd on the

ground, then force the anarchist out over an uninhabited stretch of land. By the time the pilot had been able to do this, Colonel Dawson had pulled up information on the range of the policeman's standard-issue compression gun as well as a diagram of a balloon similar to the one Rani and the anarchist were in.

They were close enough now to make out Rani and the young man she'd called Étienne. Étienne was no match for their own pilot, who was able to easily get within firing range. Zee had willed herself not to listen when David relayed the details of the colonel's plan, telling the policeman where to shoot to send the balloon plunging swiftly to the ground, without giving the anarchist a chance to release the biochemical spores or to return fire.

"He's getting close to the sea," David informed the colonel.

"Then get in fast and take your shot," the colonel advised. "If he releases his load over the water, it will be an ecological disaster of unimaginable proportions."

Zee was shaking. It was freezing up here. But when she looked at the policeman, she saw that he was perspiring with fear. He was young, not much older than David, and firing his weapon had clearly never been part of his career plan.

"Okay," the pilot said, "in about a minute we'll be in position."

The silence was unendurable. Then, when they were almost there, the policeman froze. "Are you sure that's the right one?" he asked Zee. "I can't—I *won't*—fire without your say-so."

She had to give the go-ahead. She knew she had to, but the minute she did, Rani's life would be over. She looked across to the other gondola, close enough now for her gaze and Rani's to meet. The intensity of their feelings formed a bridge for all that was in their hearts, and Zee felt Rani's thoughts as strong as if they were her own. *Wrong boy again. My fault, Zee. Not yours.* Never dropping her gaze, Rani kissed her fingertips and tapped them against her chest. Zee felt a tremendous throb, as if in that one gesture Rani had conveyed all her life force to Zee and set her free at the same time. *Not your fault, Zee.* Then, in one fluid movement, Rani placed her slim foot on the rail of the gondola, brought herself to standing position, and stepped off into the air. Her sari fluttered around her like a golden flame all the way to the ground.

"Shoot!" David yelled. "She's sure, and her best friend just gave up her life to prove it to you. Don't you see? Rani knew Zee would never give the go-ahead

107

with her in the gondola. That's why she jumped. So shoot, before he shoots us and releases that stuff all over Cornwall."

The policeman fired, but his shot was a second too late. The anarchist managed a volley of shots before he collapsed, and Zee reeled as the balloon started to plunge. She couldn't see what happened to the pilot, or to the policeman, but she and David stayed together and held each other all the way down.

CHAPTER SEVENTEEN

ALPHA AND OMEGA

It was Mia who found them. Zee could hear her yelling at David to wake up. Wake up, get up, and get out of there.

Zee tried to move but couldn't. She was surrounded by something firm and white. It pressed against her rib cage, forcing the air from her lungs. Even her face was covered, and she had to twist her neck just to breathe. If it hadn't been for David's hand still clutching her fingertips, she might have thought she was dead. It was the air bags, she finally realized, trapping the four of them in the tangled positions they'd fallen in. Finally,

Mia got David out of the tipped gondola, and this gave Zee enough slack to slide out as well.

"The other two?" she asked Mia.

"They'll be out for a while," Mia replied, as if she'd had something to do with it.

"Good. David, Mia's right. You have to go."

"I'm not leaving you, Zee."

"But you can't be found here. This was an anarchist attack. They'll want to interview us, and if we're found together, it will get back to Omura."

"The others will remember that there were four of us in the gondola. What will you say?"

"That you were someone I just met. That all I know about you is that your name is Reggie and you said you're from Bournemouth, or Weymouth, I don't remember. Hurry. You have to be gone before they get here."

"All right, but I'm not going back to London without you." He looked beseechingly at Mia. "Will you stay one more night, to give us cover?"

Mia rolled her eyes but agreed. She wrote a number on a scrap of paper and thrust it into Zee's hand. "Call me when they've finished with you. I'll come get you. Safer me than David."

Zee did not breathe easily until they were safely away.

The hardest part was calling Rani's parents. Zee insisted on doing it herself. She didn't want them hearing from a stranger that their daughter was dead. Pending identification by next of kin, Rani's body was being held at the hospital morgue, and Zee told the Kapoors she would meet them there. There was nothing she could do to change things, but she could at least make sure Rani's parents knew how brave their daughter was and that her courage had helped an MI5 team recover their first undetonated anarchist bomb. What they learned from it would help them trace members of the group and how they operated.

Most of the afternoon, though, was spent being interviewed by government security forces. Initially, the questions were aggressive. Since her best friend had died with an anarchist, both she and Rani were suspects. However, once the head of the investigative unit spoke to Colonel Dawson, the atmosphere changed. The questioning shifted to things she might have observed or felt, and since she was no longer a suspect, their interest in Reggie from Bournemouth disappeared as well. By the time they finished, she'd convinced them that Rani was an innocent victim and took some comfort in knowing that her friend's parents wouldn't be confronted with accusing questions about their daughter.

Even with Rani's parents, Zee didn't cry. It was only later, alone with David in his hotel room, that she felt the wires and strings that had held her together all day begin to loosen. What began as mere tears exploded into a torrent of wild, jagged sobs. If only Rani had turned down that invitation! If only, just this once, she hadn't gone off with the exciting stranger! Where was she now? Where were all the things that were Rani? And how was Zee going to live without ever seeing her friend again? The anguish of it sent her to her knees.

Zee would forever love the way David let her cry. It must have been terrible to watch, and just as bad to hear, but he didn't try to coax her out of it. Finally, when she was completely spent, he gave her his hand and pulled her to her feet.

"I think we need some dinner," he said.

They ordered from the room service wall, an expensive luxury. The wall was a mosaic of screens, each depicting an item that could be delivered to your room within ten minutes, arriving on a little glassed-in conveyer belt embedded in the wall. There were so many items it took them forever to decide what they wanted. *Okay, I'll split a General Tso's Chicken with you if we can split a malt too. What do you mean malts don't go with Chinese food? Of course they do.* David made Zee laugh in spite of herself, and while the distraction didn't take away her grief, it did remind her of the day's joy. Twenty-four hours ago, she thought she'd never see David again.

It would have been easy to go to bed content with that, but she knew she couldn't. The day had underscored the fact that life was unpredictable and could be surprisingly short. It was time to do what she had been telling herself she would do if she ever saw him again.

"We have to talk."

"I know," he said with a sigh. "There are some things I have to tell you."

"Me first," she insisted. Not because she wanted center stage but because she suspected much of what she was about to say would cancel anything he might have planned to say. "You're going to think this has something to do with today, but it's something I decided a few weeks ago."

She touched the Neptune's Tears that lay at the hollow of her throat, and heard again Mrs. Hart's admonition, *Be bold with your life.* She hadn't taken the necklace off since she'd gotten it, just as she hadn't taken off the charm bracelet with the two Buddhas that David had given her.

"When you go back to Omura, I want to go with you." The shock on his face was more than she'd bargained for. Clearly, he'd never considered the possibility. "It's the only thing that makes sense. They won't let you stay here. They've trained you, they need you there. So I'll go back with you."

"But—but I've told you what Omura's like. No art, no literature, nothing for the imagination. It's my home, and I belong to it, but you'd hate it."

"I would hate a lifetime without you more."

He stood up and began pacing back and forth. "You can't, Zee. You can't go with me."

She stood in front of him, blocking his path. He thought he'd never seen anyone made so beautiful by passion. His lovely Zee.

"Why can't I go with you?" she questioned. "You said yourself that Omura's underpopulated. They need people, families, lots of children. We could make a life there."

"No, we couldn't."

"Why not?"

"Because there is no Omura! That's what I have to tell you, Zee. The whole thing is a lie."

She was caught completely off guard. "I—I don't understand. It's on the galaxy maps. I've seen it."

"Yes, the planet you call Gliese 581 C exists, but as far as anyone knows, there's no life there. We picked it as a likely spot. Omura and everything about it is invented."

"I still don't understand," she said. "But I know that we were meant to be together, and if you can't stay here, I'll go with you when you're sent back home, wherever home is."

"You can't go with me, Zee," he said. "You can't because you're already there. The aliens—me, Mia, all of us—we aren't aliens at all. We're time travelers from a future Earth."

She was silent a long time. He watched waves of confusion break across her face as she tried to work out what he'd just told her. Finally, she looked up at him. "If you're from Earth, why are you here harvesting the art and literature? Or isn't that true either?"

"No, that's true. We're systematically copying it and sending back as much as we can."

"Why?"

He took her by the shoulders and stared straight into her eyes. "If I tell you, Zee, you have to promise to tell no one. Not your family or your friends, no one. It's a terrible promise to ask of anyone. You'll hate me for asking it of you, but I have no choice."

She leaned into him and felt his arms go around her. "Nothing could make me hate you, David. I promise to keep the secret, whatever it is."

"We're here harvesting because sometime soon there's going to be a catastrophic meteor strike on the planet. Almost everything will be destroyed, and what isn't destroyed will never be the same. In that sense, I *do* come from an alien planet. I was born on Earth fifteen hundred years from now."

Zee closed her eyes. For the first time, she felt no wall of reserve. His soul flowed into hers as freely as water running to the sea.

"How long?" she asked. "How long until the meteor hits?"

"We aren't exactly certain. Time isn't as reliable as you'd think. Within your lifetime."

"I still want to go with you," she said. "Nothing changes that." She remembered all the whispered reports of those said to be involved with aliens vanishing. "They've let others come back, haven't they?"

"Yes."

"Then that's what we'll do."

"It's not that easy, Zee."

"What do you mean?"

"Immigration isn't encouraged. The time leap is too great. Most relationships fail within the first few years. The émigrés seldom adapt. Drug and alcohol problems are frequent, as are suicide and unemployment. Homeless enclaves are cropping up."

"That wouldn't happen to us, David."

"And then there are the lists. Immigration from the past must be tightly controlled, because even small changes can alter the future. There are three lists that govern who can and who cannot immigrate. First, the Inconsequentials, those who died when the meteor struck, never had children, or produced little of value post-meteor. They can immigrate, at least theoretically, because they have no influence on the future. Second, the Researchables. This is the largest pool, people about whom nothing is known or no records survive. They are allowed to immigrate *only* if they can prove themselves irrelevant to the future. The final list is called the Essentials, people who will never be allowed to immigrate, because they make key contributions after the meteor strike."

"Those sound like good odds."

"I started the research before I left Prambanan. I've already looked you up, Zee. So far, it looks like you're on the Essentials list."

She felt a wave of desolation. Not to be with David, never to see him again . . . His arms tightened around her, holding her so close she could feel the necklace

Mrs. Hart had given her pressing against her neck, the trio of false diamonds, Neptune's Tears, making a warm spot at the base of her throat. As if Mrs. Hart herself were standing beside her, Zee heard again the last words her friend had said to her. *No matter what happens, be bold with your life. Don't settle for small.* That was the true message of Neptune's Tears. She pulled back just enough to look up at him.

"Then we'll find another way," she said fiercely. "We've come too far to lose each other now."

"But, Zee—"

"We *will* find another way," she repeated. "We're like orbiting pearls. No matter what pulls us apart, we'll always find our way back to each other."

She lifted her face to his, and in their kiss, she felt his thoughts, no longer hidden or withheld.

Maybe you're right, Zee. Maybe we'll always find a way to be together.